*Love, Amalia*

# Love,
# Amalia

**ALMA FLOR ADA**

*and*

**GABRIEL M. ZUBIZARRETA**

ATHENEUM BOOKS *for* YOUNG READERS

atheneum   NEW YORK   LONDON   TORONTO   SYDNEY   NEW DELHI

athenuem

ATHENEUM BOOKS FOR YOUNG READERS

An imprint of Simon & Schuster Children's Publishing Division

1230 Avenue of the Americas, New York, New York 10020

ATHENEUM BOOKS FOR YOUNG READERS is a registered trademark of
Simon & Schuster, Inc.

Atheneum logo is a trademark of Simon & Schuster, Inc.

For information about special discounts for bulk purchases, please contact
Simon & Schuster Special Sales at 1-866-506-1949 or
business@simonandschuster.com.

The Simon & Schuster Speakers Bureau can bring authors to your live event.
For more information or to book an event, contact the Simon & Schuster
Speakers Bureau at 1-866-248-3049 or visit our website at
www.simonspeakers.com.

Also available in an Atheneum Books for Young Readers hardcover edition

Book design by Hilary Zarycky

The text for this book is set in Caledonia.

Manufactured in the United States of America

0521 OFF

First Atheneum Books for Young Readers paperback edition July 2013

12  14  16  18  20  19  17  15  13  11

The Library of Congress has cataloged the hardcover edition as follows:Ada,
Alma Flor.

Love, Amalia / Alma Flor Ada and Gabriel Zubizarreta. — 1st ed.

p. cm.

ISBN 978-1-4424-2402-9 (hardcover)

[1. Grandmothers—Fiction. 2. Loss (Psychology)—Fiction. 3. Mexican
Americans—Fiction. 4. Family life—Illinois—Fiction. 5. Letters—Fiction.
6. Chicago (Ill.)—Fiction.] I. Zubizarreta, Gabriel M. II. Title.

PZ7.A1857Am 2012

[Fic]—dc23    2011023837

ISBN 978-1-4424-2403-6 (paperback)

ISBN 978-1-4424-2404-3 (eBook)

To the memory of Felicitas Gabaldoni de Zubizarreta,
who loved her grandchildren so dearly.

To Alma Lafuente de Ada, grandmother of my children and great-
grandmother of my grandchildren, and to the memory of Mireya
Lafuente, who although never a mother herself in the usual way,
was mother, grandmother, and great-grandmother to a whole family.

To Sherrill Brooks, Dolores Pudelski, Irene Davis, and Benicia
Zamperlini in the love for our shared grandchildren.

—A. F. A.

Any life can be changed by someone else's caring, especially when
it is given purely by choice with nothing expected in return.

With gratitude and recognition to the two gentlemen who reached
down and so wonderfully changed me with their caring over a long
period of time. I am blessed to have had you in my life and could
never repay even a fraction of your generosity and caring.

Roger Guido and Chuck Robel, thank you from myself and the
many others I have known whom you have also selflessly helped.

I will strive for the bar the example set.

—G. M. Z.

# ACKNOWLEDGMENTS

We are grateful for the contributions of our family during the creation of this book. Jessica Zubizarreta read the multiple versions, made very meaningful suggestions, and inspired some of Amalia's best actions. Hannah Brooks was always ready with editorial input. Isabel Campoy added to her unfaltering support of the writing task valuable recommendations, which enriched the characters and their lives.

We also appreciate the comments and suggestions made by these insightful readers: Lolita Ada, Mary Anderson, Sherrill Brooks, Dave Broughton, Liliana Cosentino, Mary Nieves Díaz Méndez, Pat Dragan, Sue Fox, Beverly Vaughn Hock, Valerie Lewis, Elaine Marie, Suni Paz, Julia Roure, Norma Tow, Vienna Vance, Camille Zubizarreta, and Timothy Zubizarreta. To all, our thanks.

Our gratitude to Lindsay Schlegel and Namrata Tripathi for welcoming our manuscript to Atheneum. A special recognition to Namrata Tripathi for her valuable support. It is a privilege to have her as an editor. Our thanks also to Emma Ledbetter, for the title suggestion, to Michelle Fadlalla and everyone on the efficient and enthusiastic Simon & Schuster staff, and to our agent, Adriana Domínguez.

*Mientras haya*
*quien entienda la hoja seca,*
*falsa elegía, preludio*
*distante a la primavera.*

As long as
someone understands the dry leaf,
a false elegy, a prelude
to a distant spring.

—Pedro Salinas, *Confianza*

# CONTENTS

# 1. Homemade Taffy

What is it, Amalia? Is something bothering you?"
Amalia's grandmother removed the boiling honey
from the stovetop to let it cool. Then she wiped
her forehead with a tissue and looked at her granddaughter. The light from the setting sun entered
the small window over the sink with a soft glow.
The geraniums on the windowsill added a subtle
hint of pink. "You are too quiet, *hijita*. Tell me
what's bothering you," her grandmother insisted.
"It is obvious that something is wrong."

"It's okay, Abuelita, *de verdad*. I'm fine."

Amalia tried to sound convincing, but her
grandmother continued, "Is it because Martha did
not come with you today? Is she all right?"

Going to her grandmother's home on Friday
afternoon was something Amalia had been doing
since she was little. For the last two years, since
they started fourth grade, her friend Martha

accompanied her most Fridays. Every week Amalia looked forward to the time she spent at her grandmother's house. But today was different.

Amalia paused before answering, "She is not coming back anymore, Abuelita. *¡Nunca más!*" Despite Amalia's efforts to control her feelings, her voice cracked and her brown eyes watered.

"*¿Qué pasa, hijita?* What's going on?" Amalia's grandmother asked softly, gently hugging her and waiting for an explanation.

Amalia shook her head, as she frequently did when she was upset, and her long black hair swept her shoulders. "Martha is going away. Her family is moving west, to some weird place in California. So far away from Chicago! Today she had to go straight home to start packing. It's not fair."

"That must be difficult." Her grandmother's voice was filled with understanding, and Amalia let out a great sigh.

For a while there was silence. The sunlight faded in the kitchen, and as the boiled honey cooled into a dark, thick mass, its sweet aroma filled the air.

"Shall we knead the *melcocha*, then?" Amalia's grandmother asked as she lifted the old brass pot onto the kitchen table and poured the sticky *mel-cocha* into a bowl. The thick white porcelain bowl, with a few chips that spoke of its long use, had a wide yellow rim. Once, the bowl had made Amalia think that it looked like a small sun on the kitchen table. Today she was too upset to see anything but the heavy bowl.

They washed their hands thoroughly in the sink and dried them. Her grandmother's kitchen towels each had a day of the week embroidered in a different color. Since today was Friday, the cross-stitched embroidery spelled VIERNES in *azul marino*, deep blue. Abuelita had taught Amalia the days of the week and the names of the colors in Spanish using these towels. Although her grandmother never seemed to be teaching, Amalia was frequently surprised when she realized how many things she had learned from Abuelita.

After drying their hands, they slathered them with soft butter, which prevented the taffy from sticking to their fingers or burning their skin. Then, with a large wooden spoon, Abuelita scooped some taffy from the bowl and poured it onto their hands.

As they pulled and kneaded, the taffy became

softer and lighter. They placed little rolls of amber-colored taffy on pieces of waxed paper. Amalia had helped her grandmother pull the *melcocha* many times, but she never ceased to marvel at how the sweet taffy changed color just from being pulled, kneaded, and pulled again. It transformed from a deep dark brown into a light blond color, just like Martha's hair. Thinking about Martha made Amalia frown.

Her grandmother might have seen her expression but made no comment about it. Rather, she said, "Wash your hands well, Amalita. Let's sit for a moment while the taffy cools down."

Before washing her hands, Amalia licked her fingers. Nothing tasted as good as "cleaning up" after cooking. The butter and taffy mixed together made a sweet caramel on her fingers, which was every bit as good as the raw cookie dough they "cleaned up" when she and Martha made cookies at Martha's house.

Once Amalia had washed and dried her hands, she followed her grandmother to the living room. They both sat on the floral sofa, which brightened the room as if a piece of the garden had been brought inside the house. Abuelita's fondness for the colors of nature could be seen in each room of her house.

"I know how hard it is when someone you love goes away. One moment you are angry, then you become sad, and then it seems so unbelievable you almost erase it. Then, when you realize it is true, the anger and the sadness come back all over again, sometimes even more painfully than before. I have gone through that many times."

Amalia listened closely, trying to guess who her grandmother was talking about. Was she thinking of her two sons who lived far away or her daughter who always promised to visit from Mexico City but never did? Or was she referring to her husband, Amalia's grandfather, who had died when Amalia was so young that she could not remember him?

"But one finds ways, Amalia, to keep them close," her grandmother added. And then, smiling as if having just gotten a new idea, she said, "*Ven*. Come with me." She then got up and motioned Amalia to follow her to the dining room.

Amalia just wanted to end the conversation. It was bad enough that Martha had told her that she had a surprise and it had turned out to be that Martha was moving to California very soon.

Martha's leaving sounded so definite and permanent that she hated even the thought of it. Talking about it only made Amalia feel worse. She wished she did not need to wait for her father to pick her up and could just walk home. Maybe then she could call Martha and hear her say that it all had been a great mistake and they were not moving after all. And it would all disappear like bad dreams do in the morning.

# 2. Christmas Cards

Abuelita signaled Amalia to come sit at the massive dining room table. Before she sat down, Abuelita put on a CD quietly in the background. Amalia could not remember Abuelita's home ever without some soft music. On the lace tablecloth there was a stack of Christmas cards, several red and gold leaves, and a box made of beautiful olive wood that Amalia immediately recognized. Her grandmother used that box to save the special cards and letters sent by relatives and close friends. At the bottom there were old letters neatly kept in bundles tied with ribbons. Amalia loved the feel of the old polished wood, the gentle waves that had been stroked so many times before.

"Are you writing your Christmas cards already, Abuelita? It's not even Thanksgiving!" Amalia was relieved to change the subject. "What are the dry leaves for?"

"I like writing my cards slowly," her grandmother replied as she picked up an unfinished card. "That way I can really think about what I will write on each one. There are so many things I want to say."

After a moment, almost as if talking to herself, Abuelita added, "I've made terrible mistakes in my life when I didn't think before speaking."

Amalia looked up, surprised. Abuelita always looked so calm and sure. It was almost impossible to imagine her acting foolishly.

Looking at the half-written card, Abuelita continued, "As I was telling you, one must find ways to keep loved ones close, even if they move away. This year I have decided to send a little bit of my backyard with each card. Every year at this time, my children and I had many good moments getting ready for the holidays. So I have gathered some of this autumn's leaves to remind them of those times. Look at this one!" and she held a maple leaf that had turned a deep crimson. "See how red it is? One of the things I have always loved about this house is seeing the trees change colors with the seasons.

"The same is true with the things we treasure:

They happen, bloom for a time, and then fade away. Then sometimes they may reappear again, or something else will take their place."

Holding the leaves up one by one, she added, "There is a poem I like very much. The poet says that a dry leaf is not an elegy, a song of death, but rather a prelude, a promise of a distant spring."

Abuelita almost seemed lost in her own thoughts, but then she returned to Amalia, saying, "Before writing each card, I like to read ones I received from the person to whom I am about to write. This reminds me that I am not the only one who wants to stay close. Do you want to look at some of last year's cards with me?"

"Sure, Abuelita," Amalia said, pushing back the lock of hair that kept falling in her face. She always enjoyed listening to her grandmother's stories, especially stories about their family. The distant relatives, some of whom Amalia could not remember ever meeting, came alive when Abuelita spoke about them. Even things that happened a long time ago, like the story of how her grandfather's parents had come from Mexico to Chicago, became so real when Abuelita told them that Amalia felt as if she had actually been there.

Today she did not feel much like listening, but making an effort to show some enthusiasm for her grandmother's offer, she added, "You can tell me all about the people who sent them."

Abuelita began pulling cards out of the box one by one. With each card she had something to say, and although she had spoken about these faraway relatives many times before, it seemed to Amalia that today she was adding special details to every story.

Holding a card with a picture of a lush landscape, Abuelita spoke for a while about her oldest son. Amalia's *tío* Patricio had fallen in love with a Costa Rican girl he met at the University of Chicago. Soon after they graduated they got married, and because she did not want to live far away from her family, they moved to Costa Rica.

"He was very concerned about leaving me and moving away. However, I reminded him that we, too, had moved away, and sometimes that is necessary," Abuelita said. "It's true that I gained a beautiful daughter-in-law and grandchildren, but it has been hard having my eldest child live so far from me. Yet they love each other and have a happy family, and that, Amalita, is one of life's greatest gifts. See how happy they look in this picture they took as soon as they arrived in Costa Rica."

It wasn't easy to imagine Tío Patricio and Tía Graciela as two young people in love when Amalia thought of the pictures her mother had received from them recently. In those pictures Tío Patricio was a balding man and Tía Graciela a rather proper-looking lady, but in the old photo Abuelita held, they were a handsome young couple looking adoringly at each other under a palm tree, almost like a movie poster. Abuelita gently put away the card with a pleased look on her face.

"Someday you must go to Costa Rica, Amalia, and visit them. It is an amazing place."

The next card was in the shape of a large Christmas tree and said FELIZ NAVIDAD in bold letters. Abuelita opened it and read it in silence, very slowly, as if pausing on every word.

"Your *tío* Manuel is quite a person, Amalia. When my brother, your great-uncle Felipe, said it was becoming hard for him to manage the old rancho alone, Manuel went back to Mexico, to help his uncle. Who do you know that goes back to Mexico to work on a farm? Everyone says they would like to go back someday, while the truth is,

11

most people just come here and stay. But no, not your uncle Manuel. He kept saying how important that land was for his family, and that he was not going to give it up. So even though he was born and raised here in Illinois, he went back and learned how to work the rancho. And he has done such a good job of it." Abuelita looked very pleased.

"There was a time when I was not sure your uncle would turn out as he has. He did many dumb things when he was in high school, and ended up dropping out. Your grandfather was very hard on him, and it broke my heart at the time." She paused, and for an instant Amalia could see the pain those memories brought, but then Abuelita smiled. "Yet he has managed to save our rancho. When he first talked about organic farming, people laughed at his idea, but now he is doing just great. There are no tomatoes that can compare with the ones he produces."

Amalia continued listening with interest. It was comforting to hear Abuelita retelling the familiar stories. Especially today, after Martha's announcement had shattered her, it was good to hear once again the words she had anticipated Abuelita would say, as she had on other occasions:

"Ay, *hijita*, how we loved that rancho. It was there where my brother Felipe and I were born—on the kitchen table! There was no doctor, of course . . . we were born with the help of our aunts. Who would ever have thought I would end up living so far away?

"When I married your grandfather, he knew how homesick I was for the ranch. We went back there as a couple once before we had children, and then when our children were very little we went several times during the summer. When they grew older it got harder to travel, but we all loved those visits!"

It seemed to Amalia that as her grandmother spoke of those distant memories, her eyes sparkled like the lake when the sun's rays hit it at midday.

Amalia wished Abuelita could just pick her up and hold her tightly as she used to do when Amalia was smaller, reassuring her grandchild that she belonged to something that would never change. But Amalia was bigger now, and Abuelita seemed to keep getting smaller, so Amalia just let herself feel surrounded by the warmth of her grandmother's voice.

Holding a Christmas card with a huge poinsettia,

13

her grandmother began to speak of Amalia's aunt, who lived in Mexico City and made costumes for movie and television actresses.

"Here is another one who went back. My daughter is just so in love with Mexico City. She's been fascinated by dresses ever since she was a little girl. She would draw them and color them and cut them out for her paper dolls. Each doll had quite a wardrobe. They had clothes for work and play, for traveling and for the theater, for going to dances and even for picnics. There was no end to their clothes!"

Abuelita gestured with her hands as if to encompass the huge table, and Amalia could just see it covered with colorful paper doll clothes.

"And that is why she lives in Mexico City, in the capital, *en el D.F.* She says she could never have the same opportunity in Hollywood, but in Mexico she dresses all the most famous stars."

She paused for a moment, and when she spoke again, her voice had a joyful ring to it.

"You can't imagine, *mi amor*, how your mother and her sister would play together when they were little girls. Well, you do know that's why your mother called you Amalia, so that you'd have her sister's name. They were inseparable, those two. Whether they were jumping rope or playing jacks, they spent all their time together. What they liked best, though, besides those paper dolls, were the times they spent playing in the yard. They would climb trees, play tag, build pretend castles, and imagine being princesses. In the summer, your *abuelito* would set up a small plastic pool, and they loved swimming in that pool. It was very small, but they didn't care because they had each other."

Abuelita probably would have continued telling more stories, but she was interrupted by a light knock on the door. It was already dark, and Amalia's father had come to get her.

As Amalia was leaving, her grandmother hugged her and whispered in her ear, "You will find a way to stay close to Martha."

Riding in the car, Amalia pondered her grandmother's words. They had brought back the sorrow she had been able to forget while listening to the family stories.

*Who cares about staying close?* she thought. *I don't want to care about someone who won't be here.*

# 3. Moving Away

Saturday mornings were always slow and lazy at Amalia's house. It was the beginning of the weekend, and no one was in a hurry to get up. Saturdays usually started the same way. Rocío, Amalia's mother, would play some CDs, so that the soft music filled the house. *Just like Abuelita,* Amalia always thought on waking up. *Like mother, like daughter.* But her mother preferred to play classic soft rock songs. Her mother had told her many times how excited people had been about those songs back in the sixties. Amalia still had trouble believing people would have found them so fascinating.

Rocío also liked to cook, and on Saturdays she took time to prepare a special brunch, while Antonio, Amalia's father, gathered flowers and cuttings from the yard and arranged them around the house. He always managed to make tasteful arrangements with the simplest elements their yard provided.

"Nothing is too much to make the weekend special," Antonio liked to say.

And just as her mother tried something different for the Saturday brunch and her father found ways to make the table look special, Amalia enjoyed choosing what to wear on Saturdays, to go out with Martha. They would first follow Martha's choice, either to the park or the playground at their new middle school, but then they would always end up at the library, which was Amalia's favorite place. After wearing a uniform all week, it was fun to wear whatever she wanted. Today she had come down to breakfast in the soccer jersey from her first team, and a pair of jean shorts, seeking comfort from the soft worn-out cloth. She had just sat down at the table when the phone rang.

"Please, pick it up, *cariño*," her mother said, while taking a quiche out of the oven.

As soon as Amalia heard the voice at the other end of the line, she became tense—she had not been looking forward to talking to Martha. Her friend sounded hurried and excited as she announced that she was in the car on her way over to Amalia's house. "It's the only time I'll be able to see you and say good-bye," Martha was explaining.

"But I thought you weren't leaving until three weeks from now," Amalia complained, surprised by this announcement.

"Because we're moving so far away, my mom decided we should spend the next two weeks with my grandparents in Grand Rapids," Martha said.

"But what about school?" Amalia insisted, not wanting to accept what Martha was saying.

"My parents say it won't matter if we miss a couple of weeks. Anyway, we'll be going to a new school, and everything is going to be different. They say it's important for us kids to spend time with our grandparents. Dad will stay here to pack. He'll be stuck making all the moving arrangements, but he wants me and the twins to go with Mom to see our grandparents."

Amalia did not want to hear anything more, and when Martha said, "So I'll see you in a little while," she answered curtly, "Yeah, fine, okay, see you," and hung up the phone. She rushed out of the kitchen to her room as she always did when she was upset. This time she slammed the door and sat on the rug by the window, holding her favorite pillow in her arms.

"Amalia, was that Martha?" called out her mother. She was standing at Amalia's door, still holding a dishrag in her hand. "Can I come in?"

"Sure, Mom," said Amalia. She didn't really want to talk to anyone, but she knew she had already disturbed the quiet Saturday morning by storming out of the kitchen without eating her breakfast—the least she could do was be nice to her mother!

"Want to tell me what's going on?" her mother asked gently. And when Amalia did not answer, she added, "Who's leaving?"

Amalia had not said anything to her parents the previous evening about Martha's moving away, as if by not speaking about it, it would not happen. But now it was here, in her face; Martha and her mother would be coming over in a little while.

"It's Martha, Mom, she's moving. She just told me yesterday. Her father got a new job. They are going all the way to the West Coast, to some *stupid* place in California."

Amalia knew her mother did not like her saying "stupid," but it made her feel better to say it out loud. She knew her mother had noticed but had probably decided it was not the moment to correct her.

"Oh, honey, I'm so sorry, *amor*, so sorry. You and Martha have always been such good friends. *Lo siento tanto, hijita.*"

"It's okay, really. I don't want to talk about it . . . but she's on her way here. Her mother is bringing her to say good-bye." And in a softer voice she added, "I don't even want to see her. I really don't want to talk to her."

"I think you should see her and talk to her before she leaves. You won't feel good afterward if you don't. Do you want to give her a small gift?"

"*Mamiii . . . por favor . . . ,*" Amalia complained, getting up from the rug and throwing the pillow on the bed. She knew her mother was trying to make it better for her, as she always did, but nothing was going to make *this* better.

*I don't want to* talk *about Martha, I don't want to* think *about Martha. I don't even want to* see *Martha or* hear *her say she's leaving.*

She had really tried to keep quiet about the whole thing, but what was the use of trying to be nice if people would go on and on talking about what she did not want to hear? Couldn't they just leave her alone?

Her mother hugged her, saying, "*Lo siento, cariño*, I'm truly sorry." And as she was leaving Amalia's room, she paused and added softly, "Please, come down and eat your breakfast."

Amalia was helping clear the table when Martha and her mother arrived. When Amalia's mother opened the door, Martha walked right in, saying, "What's up?" bubbly as always, her wavy blond hair swinging back and forth as she bounced across the room.

As Amalia stared at her friend, so many thoughts ran through her mind. *How can she be so carefree about all this? Doesn't our friendship mean anything to her? We're about to be separated forever. . . .*

Amalia's mother and father brought out coffee and pastries.

"Thank you." Martha's mother accepted a cup of coffee but sat on the edge of the sofa, already prepared to get up and go.

"I am afraid we have only a few minutes, but I did want to make sure Martha and I got to say good-bye to you. You have always been so nice to her that we wanted to thank you personally."

Martha's mother was addressing Amalia's parents as well as her.

"This has all been such a surprise, totally unexpected. Karl received this extraordinary offer all of a sudden and they needed an immediate answer, and the offer was so good, he couldn't refuse it. It's really all so sudden."

The words quickly tumbling out of Mrs. Johnson's mouth made Amalia think of a hail storm, except that she enjoyed the rattling of hail on the roof, while Mrs. Johnson's words were simply annoying.

"My parents are shocked that we'll be moving so far away," she continued, "because my mother doesn't like to fly. They insisted that the kids and I spend these last two weeks with them, in Grand Rapids. Poor Karl, he is going to stay here and make the arrangements for the house. He'll have to do all the packing himself. Fortunately, the company he'll be working for is paying for the movers. I have never had movers before. . . . He'll meet us in Grand Rapids, and then we'll all fly to Los Angeles from there. It'll be the first time in California for the girls and me. Of course, all the twins can think of is that they'll be going to Disneyland."

When she stopped, Amalia thought, *Finally she must have run out of hot air*, believing the talking was over. But after taking a breath, Mrs. Johnson continued, "Karl sends his regards. He's busy packing. There are many people Martha and I need to see this afternoon to say good-bye to, and we must not delay too much. Karl will appreciate us returning soon to help, especially since he is watching the twins, and they can be a handful, particularly now that they are so excited about going to California. Oh, there's simply so much to do." She leaned on the couch as if she were going to fall down from exhaustion.

*No wonder Martha doesn't care,* Amalia thought. *She is just being like her mother, who acts as if this is a happy occasion for everyone, without even noticing that it is a disaster for others.* Lost in her own thoughts, Amalia almost missed Martha's words.

"This is for you. There are some things here I want you to have. My new address is in there, so you can write to me soon. Dad promised to buy me a computer as soon as we get to California, and I'll be getting an e-mail address, and if you get an e-mail address too, we can e-mail each other." Martha handed Amalia a large, thick envelope. "It's the best card I could find. It'll make you laugh."

Amalia did not think any card could make her laugh right now. She thanked Martha, but her heart was not in it. She gave both Martha and her mother a quick hug and was relieved when they left.

*Saying good-bye stinks!* she thought as she climbed the steps to her room. Again she sat on the rug by the window, this time with an open book in her lap, although she did not read a single line.

# 4. Best Friends

Amalia could not stop thinking about Martha's leaving. Maybe it wouldn't have been so bad if they hadn't been in the same school since first grade. Along the way they got used to spending almost all their free time together. Although they were so different in many ways, no one in their sixth-grade class would doubt that they were best friends. Going to Abuelita's home on Fridays had been one of their favorite things to do together.

When Ma tha's twin sisters were born, Martha got a new bike, but since her parents were so busy with the babies, it was Amalia's father who took Martha and Amalia riding on the weekends.

Last summer they had both joined a soccer team and shared a dream that someday they would win the league championship together.

Amalia and Martha could turn anything into a game. They loved going to the library. It made them feel rich to think they could check out any book they wanted, sometimes as many as ten at a time. Soon they turned their trips to the library on Saturdays into a guessing game.

"I bet I can guess more titles than you." Martha was usually the first to issue challenges.

They looked at the books in the stacks together and took the ones that looked most interesting to one of the large tables in the middle of the room to browse through and decide which ones to check out. Each one would write on a piece of paper the titles of the five books she intended to check out, and the ones she thought the other one would check out.

"No way, you cheated," whoever lost would say.

"I get to pick the tiebreaker," would follow when the score was even.

It was hard to not burst out laughing in the library when they found out how many titles they had guessed right, oftentimes most of them.

Amalia enjoyed nature stories like *Julie of the Wolves*, *My Side of the Mountain*, and *Island of the Blue Dolphins*. And because she had a secret wish to become a writer someday, she also loved autobiographies of authors. Her favorite was Lee

Bennett Hopkins's *Been to Yesterdays*. She had read it several times, and every time she discovered something new in it.

Martha liked mystery stories and books with plenty of action. She also enjoyed books with unusual funny streaks like Lemony Snicket's A Series of Unfortunate Events and Roald Dahl's books. Lately she had begun to read books with Latino characters. *Return to Sender* had given her a new understanding of the plight of recent immigrants, who like immigrants of the past, contribute with their hard labor to develop and support this country, but unlike them are not received by a Statue of Liberty with a flaming torch and the words she had memorized for her history class: "Give me your tired, your poor, / Your huddled masses yearning to breath free . . ."

While she was moved by the book, it was not easy to talk with Amalia about it, so she half-jokingly declared: "After all, if my BFF is Latina, and I practically live in her house, I should read some books about Latinos." Although Amalia only smiled without saying anything, the comment made her feel good. Moments like this made their friendship so special.

Amalia and Martha knew each other so well and had played the library guessing game so many times that for some time it had become rather easy to guess which books the other would check out. But recently, as they found new interests and brought more books to the table, the game had become more challenging.

Amalia loved that her world could be opened up through her friend's interests, and she was amazed that she and Martha could still learn new things from each other.

# 5. A Right Hand

Amalia had a strange, empty feeling throughout the week. She followed her usual routine. She got up early for school so that her father could drive her and still get to work on time. Even though she wasn't in the mood to eat, she sat down to eat breakfast so as not to upset her mother, but when her mother asked, "Did you eat any of the eggs this morning?" she replied, "Yeah," not really remembering if she had actually eaten any of the eggs or just put them on her plate. In the car she tried to answer her father's questions. When he asked, "What do you think about the White Sox clinching the play-off spot last night?" she answered, "Yeah, probably won't win the first series." Yet nothing felt quite right. Any other year she would have been happy about just making the play-offs.

At school everything seemed the same but also felt completely different. Amalia got upset with herself every time she forgot that Martha was no longer there. She still glanced in the direction of Martha's desk whenever someone gave a funny answer or when the teacher did something unexpected, like look at the window, become silent, and smile to himself, as Mr. Sánchez used to do. Or stopped in the middle of an explanation to search frantically inside her handbag and then give a loud sigh of relief when she found whatever it was she was looking for, as Ms. Medina had done last week. She was used to exchanging looks with Martha that meant, *Isn't this weird?* or *Did you hear that?* or *I'm trying not to laugh, but remember this, we'll talk about it later.*

Sometimes she found herself waiting for Martha to walk with her to the cafeteria or gym class, and occasionally she walked to Martha's empty desk before realizing that it was pointless. Each time, she got angry and promised herself that she would not do that again. *When am I ever going to accept that Martha is gone and isn't coming back?* she complained to herself.

At home Amalia refused to speak about Martha. "Have you called Martha?" her mother asked her a couple of times, but she never answered. Finally, after a few awkward moments, her parents decided to respect her silence. But even if no one mentioned Martha, and no matter how hard Amalia tried not to think of her friend, memories of the things they had done together kept coming back to her.

Two years ago, when they were in fourth grade, Amalia had broken her right wrist while roller-skating. Initially she tried to make fun of it and had her friends write and draw on her cast, but soon afterward certain things became difficult to do without the use of her right hand.

She managed many tasks well. She could brush her teeth and her hair with her left hand, but getting her schoolwork done was a real challenge. No matter how hard she tried to write with her left hand, all she managed were scribbles. She had always been proud of her neat workbooks, and it upset her to turn in such messy work.

Martha came to the rescue. With her usual assuredness she asked Ms. Larin, their fourth-grade teacher, for permission to write out Amalia's schoolwork.

"She will dictate the answers to me," she explained.

Everyone knew Amalia was better at math

than Martha, so to be absolutely fair, she added, "I promise you, I will finish my math work *before* I ask Amalia for her answers."

Ms. Larin smiled with understanding, and for the next few weeks Martha made an effort to be neater than usual when writing Amalia's homework. The day the cast finally came off, Amalia said to Martha, "Now I really know what it means when someone says 'my right-hand person.'"

Martha smiled proudly, and Amalia added, "Anytime you need a right hand, I'll be there."

*That will never happen now,* Amalia thought. *One can hardly be someone else's right hand across a whole country.*

# 6. Peeps

One of the best times Amalia and Martha shared was a camping trip last summer. Amalia's parents had planned a trip to Michigan's Upper Peninsula for quite some time. When they finally set the date, Amalia begged, "Please, say Martha can come too. Then she and I can sleep in the tent while you sleep in the camper."

Once her parents had agreed to invite Martha, Amalia kept insisting, "Mom, when are you going to call Mrs. Johnson? Please, do it now."

When she heard that Martha's parents had given her permission to go, she could not stop jumping all over the place. But then she began to worry about all the things that could go wrong. Every day she would come up with some new fear to tell her parents.

"What if Martha's twin sisters get the chicken pox, or the measles, or the mumps, whatever those are, or something really bad?"

"What if there's an emergency at Dad's work-place?"

Or, "What if the *tíos* who are always telling you they'll come for a visit finally decide to come right now?"

Her mother kept reassuring her that all would go well. She wouldn't even finish listening to the latest possible disaster before simply repeating one of her favorite sayings: *No hay que morirse la víspera*, which means the same as "We'll cross that bridge when we come to it," but it sounded so much more graphic in Spanish: "Don't die the day before your death."

So, once they were on the road in her parents' new camper, Amalia was pleased to play anything Martha wanted to play, but was also content just singing or simply riding along.

Martha made a list of all the different type of license plates they saw, noting not only each state and its motto, but also the vanity plates. Soon they were trying to imagine the reasons behind the choice of vanity license plates, and made outra-geously funny stories to explain them.

Many times along the way they became silent admiring the dense forest and imagining all the kinds of animals that most likely lived there, protected by the tall trees and the dense shrubbery.

When they reached the state park, with its lovely lakeshore camping area, the girls insisted on pitching the tent themselves. They picked a spot under the huge trees not far from the camper, but closer to the water. They were happy to be sharing the adventure of sleeping in a tent and kept chatting in the dark.

"Shh, I hear something out there!" Amalia said to Martha.

"What is it? Do you think there are bears out there? Or maybe wolves?" Martha teased her.

"Go to sleep. NOW, or you are both going to sleep on the floor of the camper." Amalia's father's voice was quiet but stern. "There are other people trying to sleep in this campground."

"Okay, okay." Both girls giggled as they lowered their voices to whispers.

"I'm so happy you're here," Amalia said to Martha the next evening, as they watched the reflection of the moon on the water. "I've always wanted to sleep in a tent rather than in the camper. But I wouldn't have felt safe doing it alone."

Martha smiled back, although all she said was, "I'm happy to be here too."

Amalia was intent on learning how to fish and on catching something they could grill. After several attempted catches, with most of the larger fishes managing to get away, she was able to catch one large enough for the grill.

She was very proud of having provided dinner, even at the cost of having stuck a finger twice with a hook and having once hooked her father's jacket in the back.

The other nights, they barbecued hamburgers and hot dogs, roasted corn on the cob, and made too many s'mores.

Martha was enthusiastic about s'mores, and they finished all the marshmallows the second night. So on the third night they roasted Peeps.

"I don't know what I love more—warm chocolate, or marshmallows, or Peeps," Amalia said. "The melted sugar coat reminds me of the caramel on flan."

"Yes, but the Peeps' eyes look gross," cried Martha, holding up a stick with a roasted Peep.

There was no end to how many Peeps they could eat or how many songs they could sing.

It was the first time they had been together morning, afternoon, evening, and night.

. . .

After five days, Amalia felt as if they were no longer merely friends, but had become sisters.

"Go tell your mother I need her help," Amalia's father told Martha as he was lifting a pot of boiling water from the camp stove, without even noticing he was addressing Martha.

"Do you know where she is?" Martha responded, noticing his error but not wanting to correct him.

Amalia felt good about the bonding that had taken place, but she was too bashful to bring it up. After all, Martha had two younger sisters, and perhaps sharing time like this had not been quite as important to her.

It certainly had been very special to Amalia, who had always longed for a sister. She remembered the pain they all had felt when her mother had twice lost a baby near birth.

So, although she did not say anything, she held on to the nice feeling of sharing this time with Martha, as if indeed they were sisters.

"Let's stop for lunch," Rocío suggested as they approached the town of Holland in Michigan's Lower Peninsula. "One of my best friends in college was from here," she explained when they arrived in the town. "Her family was descended from the first Dutch people who settled here. With those blue eyes and your light hair, you could also be a descendant of a family like hers, Martha." Amalia's mother added, "Do you know where your ancestors were from?"

"Well, my parents say we have some Irish, and German, and Scottish, and English in our background. But it is all so confusing. It doesn't really feel like we came from any place in particular," Martha answered. And then, with her usual cheerful tone, she added, "Maybe someday I'll dig up my ancestry. It would be a cool project." And a broad smile lit her face.

After they had spent some time touring the main street, re-created to provide a Dutch flavor, Amalia and Martha entered a souvenir shop.

"I'll bet you can't guess what I'm going to get my mother," Martha challenged Amalia.

"Hmmm." Amalia looked around, trying to remember the things Martha had looked at as they browsed the store. "I get three questions."

"Okay. But only yes or no," replied Martha, looking in all directions, so as not to give Amalia any clues.

"If I squeeze it really hard, can it be smaller than a softball?"

"Nope."

"I guess it's not a scarf, then."

Martha kept looking all around.

Amalia smiled. "Are you buying more than five of the same thing?" she said, knowing that she had guessed right.

Martha laughed and grabbed a bag of a dozen red tulip bulbs.

"I could have even told you they would be red. Because I know you always get your mother red things."

"Well, it's her favorite color anyway." Martha reached for a second bag of red bulbs. "And you're thinking you want some for your mother too. And you'd spend forever trying to decide which color to get her. But since I have the red ones, you'll want the same so we can remember this trip."

Both girls laughed while they continued to look for some small souvenirs, Martha for her sisters, Amalia for Abuelita.

For lunch Rocío encouraged them to order the split pea soup she was having, assuring them it was delicious. It looked too green and weird with small pieces of ham floating on it, and Martha could not be convinced. Amalia was feeling so happy that it was easy for her to agree with her mother, and when she tasted the soup, she decided that either her mother was right after all or simply that being happy made anything, even split pea soup, taste good.

At the restaurant's gift shop, while the girls looked at the books and postcards that showed the tulip fields in spring, Amalia's mother came to them and said, "Doesn't it seem impossible to have so many flowers in a field?" And then she promised, "We'll make a special trip next spring so you two can see the tulips in full bloom. It will be an amazing sight. Something one never forgets."

The girls looked at each other and smiled, knowing that even if they did not come back, they would have at least two dozen red tulip blooms to enjoy next spring.

How would that ever happen now?

# 7. Without Saying Good-Bye

The large envelope Martha had given Amalia lay unopened on her desk for three days. Each evening while doing her homework, Amalia picked up the envelope. It was heavy, and she wondered what was inside. But she was not about to open it. What good would that do?

On Thursday evening Amalia took the thick envelope and tucked it away in the bottom of a drawer. She was not going to open it and did not want to keep looking at it.

That night she promised herself that the next day when she was at her grandmother's house, she would have a good time and not even think of Martha. She would ask her grandmother to show her how to make pineapple or coconut flan with the secret family recipes that Abuelita had promised to teach her one day. And she would ask her for stories of growing up in Mexico.

*I'll never remember the names of all those places and people. I'll have to ask Abuelita to retell the stories again and again so I can remember them all,* she thought as she got into bed. She went to sleep peacefully for the first time that week.

Friday started like any other Friday. Halfway through the afternoon, while Amalia was in art class, Dr. Guerrero, the school principal, appeared at the classroom door. He signaled to Mrs. Frazen to come out to the hallway. After telling the students that she expected their best behavior, Mrs. Frazen left the class. Somehow Amalia's classmates seemed to sense something was seriously wrong and stayed quietly in their seats.

When Mrs. Frazen came back into the classroom, she went directly to Amalia's desk and asked her to take her things and meet Dr. Guerrero, who was waiting for her in the hallway. Amalia was both surprised and concerned when the principal asked her to accompany him to the office. What could possibly be wrong? As they turned the corner in the hallway, Amalia saw her father. He rushed to her, opened his arms, and held her tightly.

"You have to come, darling. It's your *abuelita*. She is at the hospital."

"What happened? What's wrong?"

There was no easy answer her father could give her. Something was wrong with her grandmother, and they had taken her to the hospital in an ambulance.

"Let's go see her now, please!" Amalia cried.

"That's what we're doing. Your mother is on her way there too," he replied. But before they reached the hospital, they got a call from Amalia's mother.

Even before her father said anything, Amalia knew something bad had happened. She had never seen her father's face look so strained, and she realized he was containing a sob.

Then he turned onto a quiet street. He stopped the car and opened his arms to Amalia, and holding her tight, said, "Abuelita is gone. She has just died. Her heart had stopped shortly after she reached the hospital."

Amalia let her father hold her for a moment, but then she pulled away. "I didn't get to say goodbye," she cried. "It's not possible. She can't be gone without even saying good-bye."

While her father continued driving toward the hospital, Amalia tried to control her sobbing, but she could not stop thinking, *Without even saying good-bye*.

## 8. Different Smells

We can't go and leave her here." Amalia wasn't sure what would happen now, but leaving while her grandmother's body was in the hospital did not feel right.

"*No te preocupes*, don't worry," her father said. "It's all taken care of."

"It's okay, *mi hijita*," was all her mother could say as she wrapped her arms around Amalia while they walked out of the hospital.

They had stayed in the hospital for what seemed like a very long time, but it was still twilight as they drove home. It was not a long drive, but it felt as if they would never arrive. When they finally did, Amalia's mother suggested that she take a warm shower, drink some milk, and go to bed.

"It's so dark outside." Amalia was looking out of her bedroom window when her mother entered.

"There's no trace of the moon, and not a single star."

"Come, get into bed," said her mother. At that moment her father also entered the room, and they tucked her in together, something they had not done in years.

Her mother held out a cup of tea.

*"Tómatelo, tómatelo,"* she said, encouraging Amalia to drink the fragrant combination of *manzanilla y tila*, and waited until she drank it all, hoping the chamomile and linden blossoms would help her relax.

"Abuelita used to give me this . . ." Amalia could not finish the sentence.

*"Sí, mi hijita, tómatelo,"* both her parents repeated as they stayed with her, one at each side of her bed, until she finally fell asleep.

She did not wake up until late morning, and she felt totally exhausted, as if instead of sleeping she had been running for hours.

*"¿Mami?"* She lay in bed, calling out, but not wanting to get up.

*"¡Mamáaa!"* She wished she were still asleep and that someone would wake her up and tell her that yesterday had all been a bad dream. *Abuelita cannot be dead. It is a mistake!* she kept thinking.

*Mami will come in and tell me everything is all right.*

"*¿Cómo estás, hijita?*" Only her father was at home, and he had come when he heard her call out. He gave Amalia a long, warm hug and encouraged her to get dressed and come down.

A few minutes later he came up to her room again.

"You need to eat," he insisted as he led her to the brunch he had prepared.

"Stop poking at your food. Eat something, *hijita.*" Her father was also staring ahead and could have been talking to her or not. Amalia kept finding it impossible to accept the truth and certainly did not feel like eating.

"Okay," she murmured as she kept moving the food around on her plate. It seemed impossible that everything had changed so drastically, that her *abuelita* would never be there for her anymore.

"As soon as you are ready, we will go to your grandmother's house. That's where all the family is getting together," her father said, trying to force a smile, but Amalia could see there was a great sadness in him.

• • •

"We're here." Her father broke the silence of the ride, and Amalia suddenly realized they had arrived at Abuelita's large two-story house.

Amalia felt as if she were in a totally different place. It had been less than a day since she had driven home with her parents from the hospital, and yet it seemed as if her whole life had changed overnight.

"Let's go inside now." Her father put his arm around Amalia and pushed her a little as he realized she was not moving toward the house. He continued holding her as they walked up the few creaking steps to the porch.

There were a lot of people inside the old house, all of whom seemed to be talking at the same time. Her grandmother always had nice music quietly playing in the background, music that always seemed to soften what was said. Now, with no music, even though people were trying to speak softly, Amalia felt there was a lot of noise, more than she had ever before experienced in that house.

"We must be thankful that she died so peacefully and didn't suffer," Amalia heard her mother say as she hugged a tall woman dressed in black and wearing higher heels than Amalia had ever seen.

Without makeup and with red, swollen eyes and disheveled hair, the woman did not look like the pictures in the family album, or the photograph her mother kept on top of her dresser, but nevertheless Amalia realized she was looking at Tía Amalia, her mother's sister after whom she had been named.

The sisters had initially looked composed, as they made an effort to remain calm, but suddenly they embraced each other, crying.

"¡Ay, Malia, Malia!" her mother keep repeating.

"¡Ay, Rocío, mi hermana!" was the reply that followed each sob.

As Amalia observed her mother and aunt crying in each other's arms, they seemed to become younger and younger, as if through their tears they were being changed into the two inseparable little girls her grandmother had always talked about.

Amalia was fascinated by the transformation. From the moment she had seen her at the hospital, her mother had seemed very strong and in control. She had hugged Amalia for a long while, but then turned to her husband and began to talk about making the funeral arrangements.

Only for a moment had she seemed about to break down, while she held on to Amalia's father, saying, "*Toño, ¡ay, Toño!* How could this happen?" But when a nurse came in to tell her that the hospital's director was ready to speak to her, she pulled herself together again and went out with the nurse.

Amalia stayed with her father while her mother spoke to the hospital director and then went to make all sorts of calls, first to her brothers and sister and then to other relatives and some close friends. Her mother had become almost like a robot, working faster and faster as if she were stuck in high gear.

"We will have the funeral next Monday, as soon as the family is all here," Amalia's mother had announced on the drive home. "I just talked to Amalia and Manuel. They will call Patricio." These were the only words she said during the ride home, although she had sat in the backseat with Amalia and had held her hand during the entire ride. When they'd arrived home, she remained calm and seemed more concerned about Amalia's feelings than her own, but Amalia felt that with each moment her mother became more distant and withdrawn. Now, in her sister's presence, she had finally broken down.

But she did not continue looking at her mother and aunt for too long. More people kept dropping in, and they all seemed to want to talk to someone. Each person who arrived would start the same process of questions and answers, which Amalia did not want to hear over and over.

"*Antonio, ¿dónde está Amalita?* Where is my niece?" she heard a tall man wearing faded jeans and cowboy boots ask her father. He was taller than everyone else in the room, and he tried to coax a smile to his face, just as Amalia's father had done, while he added, "She must greet her *tío* Manuel."

Amalia felt intimidated by this large man with the deep voice. She wanted to turn around and find a place to hide, but this was the son Abuelita was so proud of—the son who had been willing to return to Mexico to save the family ranch. She made an effort to give him a shy smile in response, but somehow she could not control herself anymore and broke out crying.

Tío Manuel put his arms around her and gently moved her from the crowded living room into a quieter spot in the dining room.

"I know you were the apple of her eye. She was so proud of you, and you gave her so much joy. That is what you must think about now." Amalia heard the gentle words spoken in the deep voice, but she could not truly register their meaning. Abuelita was gone, forever. What did anything else matter?

She stared out of the window as a light rain began to fall. Every minute there were more friends and relatives in the house.

*"Hay un taxi en el* driveway," she announced, not sure if anyone had heard her.

A taxi was idling outside the house, and a tall man and the taxi driver were standing next to it. It looked like the driver was demanding something from the man.

"Someone is in the driveway," she said, and motioned to her father, who was already headed toward the front door with his wallet in his hand.

Her *tío* Patricio and her *tía* Graciela had arrived in an airport taxi with Amalia's cousins Julián and Lucía.

"He wouldn't take a credit card," Tío Patricio explained.

Her father made sure that Amalia greeted

them, but she was relieved when after Tío Patricio and his family had kissed her, they all rushed to be with Tío Manuel. The two brothers held each other in a tight embrace, and Amalia could see they were both weeping.

The light rain had now become a storm, and as the water poured over roofs and trees, neighbors came pouring into the house. It seemed as if each one was bringing more and more food—enchiladas, tamales, frijoles, *arepas*, *arroz con gandules*, and *arroz con pollo*—food as diverse as their neighborhood. Someone had put a large pot of *menudo* soup on the stove. New smells from all the food filled the house, so different from the sweet smell of taffy she remembered so well.

To Amalia it seemed impossible that little more than a week ago she had been pulling the delicious *melcocha* with her buttered hands, while her grandmother's favorite songs played softly, sharing the joy of making the dark honey turn lighter and lighter, and feeling the satisfaction of having created something, even if that something was only pieces of candy placed on waxed paper.

Trying to recover that moment, Amalia went into the kitchen, where she saw the embroidered kitchen towels that her grandmother always kept so neat, lying wrinkled and scattered on top of the table, their different colors and the days of the week—LUNES, JUEVES, DOMINGO, MARTES—all mixed up in no order.

*Nothing will ever make sense in this house anymore,* Amalia thought. She felt the pain of her loss with the full realization that everything would be forever different. It hit her almost like a punch, creating a sharp pain in her chest and a feeling that she could not breathe. She ran out of the kitchen, where she had spent so many hours with her grandmother, onto the back porch and could not stop crying.

She felt no comfort from seeing that others also felt pain, nor could their nice words console her. She felt awful—and no matter what happened, the feeling only became worse.

While so many people had gathered in her grandmother's house, all trying to share feelings and offer support to one another, Amalia felt as if no one could ever understand her or share her pain. What she was feeling was hers and hers alone. It was *her* life that did not feel right anymore, *her* life that would have a huge void from having had her grandmother taken away from her.

# 9. Lucky?

During the next days, Amalia felt as if she were walking in a dream. Her parents insisted she stay home from school all week, saying it would be good for her to spend some time with her cousins. Even though only Aunt Amalia was staying in their guest room, the house felt like a busy train station. While Tío Manuel and Tío Patricio and his family were staying at her grandmother's house, everyone came in and out of Amalia's house constantly, since that was where they all gathered for meals.

Amalia went from room to room, not able to sit still and not wanting to stay with anyone too long.

She heard over and over people telling her, "*¡Ay, querida!* Oh, sweetheart." Her aunt and uncles hugged her, and Tía Graciela insisted on kissing her. "*Lo siento tanto.* I'm so sorry."

"*Lo sé.* I know," she would say to remove herself from almost any situation.

Her cousin Lucía asked her many questions about school and life in Chicago, but she could only give the shortest answers. Having never been in the United States before, Lucía found many things fascinating and kept comparing everything with what she had seen in movies and TV shows. She wanted to explore the city and go places with her parents. They always asked Amalia to join them, but Amalia never found the heart to do so.

"*No gracias, hoy no*. I don't feel so good. Maybe *mañana*."

Thankfully, her cousin Julián seemed to only want to hang out with their *tío* Manuel, helping him make repairs inside Abuelita's house.

When her mother commented, "My mother never wanted to remodel the house since my father died, but some changes will need to be made if it is going to be rented out," Amalia rushed outside without even stopping to get a coat. She did not want to hear any more. New people living in the house she had always considered another home was more than she could handle.

A while later, her cousin Lucía commented, "We only saw Abuelita twice, the two times she came to visit, but I really enjoyed being with her. She was so nice."

*Only twice and nice.* What could Amalia said to that? Lucía seemed to be waiting for an answer, but when Amalia remained silent, she wandered away to ask her mother to take her shopping.

Her cousin had explained earlier that she wanted to take advantage of being in the United States to shop in the malls.

"You have so many great stores close by," she would constantly say, and she rarely spoke of anything else but the things she had seen already and wanted to buy and the choices she was trying to make.

"Why don't you come with us?" she asked Amalia one more time, when she and her mother were ready to leave.

*No.* Mi abuelita *died and I don't feel like shopping,* was all that came to mind, but Amalia shook her head and did not say anything.

"You were lucky that you lived so close to Abuelita," said Julián. Although he was only two years older than Amalia, he was very tall and looked almost like a grown-up.

"The stories she told were really interesting,"

Julián continued. "Especially about our grand-father—how he was born in Chicago because his parents had come here looking for work. Abuelita was so proud of them. She told us that Abuelito's father, our great-grandfather Nicolás, had arrived as a farmworker but then decided to open a store. Abuelito's mother, María, had been working in a garment factory. But it was hard work in those sweatshops, and Abuelito felt that if they worked together in the store they could make it succeed. And they truly did. It seems that it was more than a store. They had a few tables in the back where they would serve food, and all the neigh-bors would gather there to share news in the eve-nings. Not everyone in those times knew how to read and write, but Great-Grandma María did, and she would write letters for the people to send home and would read the replies they received. And so when our grandfather grew up, he was able to go to college, and that's how he became a surveyor.

"Yeah, I wish I could have heard many more of those stories," Julián added, and then, smiling at Amalia, he insisted, "You really were lucky."

• • •

To Amalia, all this talk about being lucky sounded crazy. How could anyone talk about being lucky when Abuelita had just died? And everyone talked so naturally about Abuelita in the past tense, almost as if she were something that had been discarded, like an old, worn sweater or a threadbare quilt. Why weren't they as overwhelmed as she was by the loss of someone so special who loved them so much?

That same morning she had woken up thinking, *I need to ask Abue how come she never told me that after Tío Manuel moved to Mexico he grew a mustache as big as Zapata's.* Emiliano Zapata was the leader of the Mexican Revolution whose photo Amalia had seen in a book about the history of Mexico. She could imagine her grandmother's smile as she would say, *Sí, hijita,* just like Zapata's! But then she realized that she would never be able to ask her grandmother anything again, and she stayed in bed crying for a long time.

# 10. Abuelita's Kitchen

Whenever Amalia was alone, thoughts of Abuelita filled her mind.

She would find herself wishing she could ask her grandmother, *What will we bake today?* Or, *Did you get any new letters from Mexico?*

She could almost hear her *abuelita*'s reply: *Let's see, what would you like to bake?* Or, *Shall I tell you what your* tía *Amalia just wrote?* Remembering her distinct voice so clearly lifted her spirits for a moment. But then she would realize her grandmother was gone, and she would feel her heart sink.

During the day, she would keep busy, and her parents continued to be very supportive.

"Are you okay?" her mother asked.

"Yes, Mom, I'm okay," was always her reply.

"Do you need anything? Shall I drive you someplace?" her father offered.

"I'm good, thanks," she'd say.

But she knew she did not feel okay. The problem was that there was no way to tell anyone what she needed, because what she needed was her grandmother, and no one could give her that.

Every night her parents tucked her in and lingered in her room until she fell asleep, exhausted. In the mornings she would wake up very early and would stay in bed pretending to be asleep, with the memories of her grandmother swirling in her head, like scenes from a movie. Playing those moments over and over in her mind was the only thing she truly wanted to do.

The more she replayed those scenes in her head, the more Amalia realized that time shared with her *abuelita* was more than a nice time creating wonderful treats or sharing family stories; Abuelita had provided her with a sense of belonging. There was a time in particular that Amalia remembered now, a time when she had been very troubled and felt trapped in a problem. She had thought and thought about how to undo something she had done and had finally decided to talk to her grandmother about it.

Two years ago, before Martha began accompanying her to her *abuelita's* home, Amalia arrived one Friday feeling very confused and did not know how to approach her grandmother. She spent longer than usual working on her homework, but finally she gathered enough courage and said, "Abuelita, I want to talk to you about something."

Without making any comments, Abuelita disregarded the ingredients she had been setting out in the kitchen to make chocolate cake and instead filled one of her cut-crystal glasses with mango juice. Amalia was surprised, because her *abuelita* used those glasses only on special occasions. Then Abuelita placed the glass along with a cup of coffee and some cookies on a serving tray lined with one of her embroidered napkins, and in a very adult tone invited Amalia to go sit with her on the sofa.

After placing the juice on the coffee table in front of Amalia, her *abuelita* said softly, "Would you like to tell me what is bothering you so much?"

At first Amalia could not find her voice. She felt both ashamed and unhappy about what she was holding inside. But she also felt relieved. By treating her as she might one of her adult guests, Abuelita had made Amalia feel grown up.

In a way it comforted her, but it also made her feel worse about disappointing her grandmother, and it took her some time to begin speaking. Finally she said, very softly, with her eyes downcast, "One of my friends has done something wrong, and she doesn't know how to undo it." After a brief pause, she added, "I don't know how to help her."

Abuelita patted Amalia's hand, saying, "If you talk about what has happened, maybe you will begin to find a solution."

Amalia then told her, with shame in her voice, "My friend has taken something that did not belong to her. She did not mean to keep it, but now she cannot put it back. She wants me to help her, but I really don't know what to do." Her voice broke down, and her eyes got moist.

"Even if what happened can't be undone, tell me what would be the best solution," her grandmother said.

"The best thing would have been for her not to take it in the first place."

"Although it's not possible to go back in time, tell me why this would have been the best idea. In thinking about why, you may find the answer."

"Well, it would be good because the person

whose stuff she took would have it back. And no one would feel bad."

"Well, it seems to me you have your answer."

Abuelita took a sip of her coffee and a bite of a snickerdoodle she and Amalia had baked the week before from a school recipe.

After some silence, she continued. "What is it that your friend took, and from where?"

By then Amalia was sure her grandmother knew they were talking about her and not a friend. So, after thinking for a moment, she said, "I took some DVDs from school. They were in a box at the end of a hallway past the principal's office and the library."

As soon as the words were out of her mouth, Amalia felt as if a weight had been lifted from her chest, a weight that had made her feel so bad for two long days. So she continued speaking at a faster pace: "No one ever goes there. I don't know why the box was there. I thought I could take them, watch them, and put them back and nobody would notice."

"I see. Were they new DVDs?"

"Yes. They are new," Amalia answered. "Once I realized that only the top one was open and the others had never been opened, I didn't open them. They are about the history of sports. I have them right here in my backpack. They probably belong to Ms. Neves, our coach," she added with even more shame, looking at her shoes.

"Was there anyone else with you when you took them?"

"No. There was no one," Amalia said confidently.

"Well then, what should be the next step?"

Amalia wished her grandmother had not asked that. She realized she had hoped that her grandmother was going to make the problem disappear, but that wasn't going to happen. It was her problem. And she was going to have to solve it.

There was another long pause.

"Do you think I need to go to the principal?"

"Well, it seems to me you could explain the situation to her, just like you explained it to me."

Amalia could not imagine herself speaking to the principal. She had known Mrs. Armas since she started school in first grade but had never spoken to her directly. And although the principal seemed a nice person, she was also very strict.

"Oh . . . I don't think I can do that."

They both remained silent for a while. Amalia felt very disappointed. Speaking to the principal was a very hard thing to expect her to do, so once again she tried to see if her *abuelita* could take care of the problem.

She asked, "Couldn't you take them to Mrs. Armas, please?"

Amalia tried to use her most endearing voice, but her grandmother looked at her without a smile. "You took the DVDs, Amalia. You need to face the principal."

Amalia looked down once more, and then heard her grandmother say, "But I'll tell you what. I will go with you. Leave the DVDs with me. I will meet you after school on Monday and we will go to your principal's office together."

Amalia gave a big sigh. Going to see the principal terrified her, but with Abuelita there, it would be easier to do.

"Are you going to tell my parents, Abuelita? Please don't."

"No. I'm not going to tell them . . . at least, not for now. First let's see how the talk with your principal turns out."

Just then they heard knocking at the kitchen door.

"Am I early?" Amalia's father asked as he noticed all the cake ingredients sitting unused on the kitchen counter and no familiar smell of baking.

"No, we were just finishing up," Abuelita said as she started putting the cake ingredients away. "Maybe Amalita should come over Monday afternoon. I can pick her up from school."

"Why, is something wrong?" he asked as he helped himself to some of the Mexican chocolate Abuelita used for baking.

"No, things are going very well," she answered calmly. "On Monday, Amalia and I can finish the cake, and there will be some for you to take home also." Sensing that he suspected something, she added, "It will be the strawberry dulce de leche cake you love so much."

Amalia's father smiled happily. Abuelita's cakes were all delicious, but the special vanilla cake, layered with strawberries and dulce de leche, that Abuelita made each year for his birthday was his favorite. It would be a special treat precisely because it was not his birthday.

Finishing his piece of chocolate, he replied, "Okay, I will pick her up from here after work on Monday."

Amalia hugged her grandmother and, after thinking for a moment, said, "Your kitchen is the best place in the world, Abuelita."

# 11. Give and Take

On Monday her grandmother was waiting outside Amalia's last class when the bell rang.

"Shall we go?" she asked.

Amalia could think of a thousand places she would like to go to, and none of them included the principal's office, so all she said was, "I guess so."

It would have been difficult for her to describe just how she was feeling. Throughout the weekend she had worried about this moment. Now her grandmother was there, so she was not terrified, but she was still afraid, not sure how things would turn out, and she had a queasy feeling as if she had eaten too much, although she had hardly been able to touch her lunch.

"Doing the right thing is not always easy, and you are not guaranteed of the result," Abuelita told her as they walked down the hall.

Then they were in the office, and the secretary

called the principal to let her know they were there. Amalia thought the secretary, who was always so nice, was giving her a stern look, and she lowered her eyes.

Amalia was feeling more uncomfortable each minute. When Mrs. Armas opened the door and said, "Come in, please, sit down," Amalia sat on the edge of the chair, in silence, not knowing what to say or what to do.

"I understand, Amalia, that you have done something you are sorry about." Amalia was relieved that the principal's tone was intended to make her feel at ease. But when she added sternly, "Do tell me about it," Amalia's confidence disappeared.

She noticed the DVDs on top of Mrs. Armas's desk, and it was clear that her grandmother had already had a discussion with the principal. *So she already knows. Why do I have to talk about it?*

The last thing she wanted was to have to speak about the issue. She looked up at her grandmother, but her grandmother remained silent.

"I did something very stupid, Mrs. Armas. I don't really know why I picked up those DVDs," she began.

Realizing that the principal wanted her to keep speaking, and not knowing what else to say, Amalia added an apology. "I am sorry. I am really sorry."

"I know you are sorry, Amalia, as well you should be; however, that is not enough."

For a moment there was silence, until Amalia said very softly, "What do you want me to do?"

"There are three steps to complete when one makes a mistake. The first is to apologize, the second is to fix the problem, and the third is to learn how not to repeat the same mistake. That way we take responsibility for our actions, and also learn from our mistakes."

"Yes, Mrs. Armas." Amalia's voice was so low it could hardly be heard.

"I'll tell you what you can do." Mrs. Armas paused for a moment. It was just an instant, but long enough for ideas of all the possible punishments she had been dreading to flood Amalia's mind.

"Please don't tell my parents," she pleaded, fighting to keep the tears out of her eyes.

"Your grandmother and I have already discussed that," said Mrs. Armas, "and since you are going to take responsibility and your grandmother is supporting you, for now we will not tell your parents.

"You have apologized to me, and I accept that. Now tell me how you are going to fix your mistake and how you are going to learn from it."

Amalia thought back to the conversation with Abuelita and what the principal had just said. "I guess I have to return the DVDs to Coach Neves."

The principal looked at her, waiting, until Amalia added, "And apologize for what I did."

"That will be a good start. In this case, returning the DVDs unopened pretty much takes care of the damage you have done. Can you imagine a situation where having taken them, even for a day, would have created a problem?"

Amalia thought about the DVDs. They were a collection on the history of sports. She had been attracted by the topic, so after thinking for a moment she said, "Yes, if Coach Neves had planned to show one of them on the day that I took them. She had said she had a surprise for us." At that point Amalia was making an effort not to cry.

"Why do you suppose you did not think of that before you took the DVDs?" Although the principal was very serious, she seemed to be encouraging Amalia to speak.

Amalia looked down. She was ashamed of what she had done, and embarrassed for not having thought of the consequences. "I guess I did not think about much," she replied. Her voice continued to be very soft.

"Actually, you probably thought about many things . . . about how much you wanted those DVDs, about whether you would get caught. What you did not do was to think about others." Now the voice of the principal expressed her disappointment.

"I don't know why I didn't think about Coach Neves. I really like her, and I love PE."

"What you have done could get you a serious punishment." Mrs. Armas paused for a moment. Amalia thought about what a serious punishment could be and felt terrified again. Then she heard the principal say, "But I believe that having you think about this will be more useful to you.

"The consequences of our acts are long-lasting. This is why I want you to reflect on how thinking of others when we are about to do something we know is wrong can help us avoid making that mistake."

The principal stopped for a moment. Amalia waited, anxious to hear what would come next.

"I am going to try out something with you," Mrs. Armas said, and then explained, "I want you to think about three completely different situations where, no matter how sorry you would be for having done something wrong, you could not undo the damage."

Amalia looked at the principal expectantly. Was that going to be all? Then she heard Mrs. Armas add, "I want you to write an essay about each situation. Your essay must show why it is important to think of the consequences of doing things you know are wrong. Bring the first essay to my office next Monday, and one on each of the following two Mondays. Then we will talk again."

Amalia's head was spinning. What a relief! The principal was not going to tell her parents. She was not going to be suspended. No one, besides the coach, needed to know what she had done. She immediately began thinking about the possible topics for the essays. Then she noticed that her grandmother was looking at her sternly, and she realized she must thank the principal.

"Thank you, Mrs. Armas," was all Amalia could

think of saying, but realizing how lame that was, she added, "Thank you very much."

Walking to her grandmother's home, trying to keep up with Abuelita's brisk steps, Amalia could only think, *I'm so lucky to have Abuelita*. And for the first time in several days her heart felt light and joyful.

When they got to her home, Abuelita reminded Amalia that there was one more thing to be done that day. While Amalia washed and sliced the large strawberries Abuelita took out of her refrigerator, her grandmother chose a CD to play. Upon hearing the first notes, Amalia recognized one of Abuelita's favorite songs, "*Gracias a la vida*." She listened to the words of the song:

> *Gracias a la vida*
> *que me ha dado tanto . . .*
> Thanks to life
> that has given me so much . . .

She looked at the bright red of the strawberries and licked some dulce de leche that had ended up on her wrist. She then spread the dulce de leche on one of the two vanilla cake layers her grandmother had baked that morning and placed the strawberry slices on the dulce de leche. Her grandmother placed the other cake layer on top and watched while Amalia spread some dulce de leche on the cake top and on its sides and placed more strawberries to cover the dulce de leche.

When Amalia finished and looked up, she saw the bright smile on her *abuelita*'s face and thought, Gracias a la vida *for strawberries, for dulce de leche, and for Abuelita's smiles.*

By the time her father came to pick her up, the best strawberry dulce de leche cake was waiting for him.

# 12. When Something Can't Be Undone

That next Friday, Abuelita had a plate of cookies already baked and covered with aluminum foil on the kitchen table.

"Today we will not cook. I want you to use all the time to write your essay," was the first thing Abuelita said after hugging Amalia.

"Well, I've been thinking all week about what to write," Amalia said. Taking a notebook out of her backpack, she sat at the kitchen table and began to work.

She wrote about taking something you know you should not and meaning to return it, but then the object breaks and there is no way to return it.

After she finished, she read her grandmother the draft.

Abuelita approved of Amalia's idea but suggested she add more details.

"Mrs. Armas has given you an opportunity; you can choose what you make of it. If you do your best, you will never regret it."

"But how do I do that?"

"Write with your heart. It can recognize what is right and what is wrong, and it can also guide you. Don't be afraid to feel what you are writing about."

Amalia was not looking forward to a major writing task. She was content with having thought of a good idea. That was all that Mrs. Armas had asked for. But obviously Abuelita did not think so. Then she remembered that the principal had really trusted her, had not given her any of the awful punishments she feared, and had not told her parents. So she reread what she had written and thought more about it. First she tried to add to what she had written, but then she put the paper aside and started again. She wrote slowly, stopping to think several times, until she felt she had something ready to show to her grandmother.

"This is so much better," said her grandmother when she read the final draft. "I think you only need to explain a little better how the boy truly felt after his neighbor's toy broke."

Amalia gave a deep sigh. She so much wanted to be finished . . . but she took her pencil and continued writing.

The following Friday, Amalia brought her composition already written. She did not want to waste all her time at Abuelita's with these assignments. She had written about a girl who took a bracelet from another girl's locker. But then someone else stole the bracelet from her.

Abuelita did not seem as pleased with her writing as Amalia had hoped she would be. She commented, "I think this will work for this second time. But you can't continue going on with the same idea of taking something and being unable to give it back. Your two compositions so far are two versions of the same topic."

Amalia was truly disappointed. She had put in a lot of effort this time and had added all kinds of nice details. But she realized her grandmother was right, so she listened to what Abuelita had to say.

"Now think beyond. There are many other actions we can do that even if we are sorry afterward we won't be able to undo."

"You mean, like killing someone?"

"Well, I wouldn't go into something so dramatic. Let's stay at the level of things an ordinary person, you for instance, could easily do."

"¡Ay, Abuelita! You are making this hard!" Amalia complained.

"Really, Amalita? I thought I was making it easy."

The third week Amalia sat down to write as soon as she got to her grandmother's house. She had brought an outline and wrote about the damage done by gossiping, saying something untrue about someone or something true but private. She even tried to come up with an image. When she'd thought of two, she used one at the beginning of the essay, saying that spreading gossip is like spilling a glass of milk on the ground, and ended by saying that finally it is like blowing dandelion seeds into the air: No one knows where the seeds will fall and a new dandelion plant will grow.

After she had turned in all three essays, Mrs. Armas called Amalia to her office.

"I have been very pleased reading your essays, Amalia," she said, and then asked her, "How did you feel about writing them?"

"It's been a hard time for me. I have never kept a secret from my parents. At times I wished I could just go to them and explain what has been going on. But I was so afraid they'd be disappointed in me. On top of that, it has not been easy to find a way to say what I wanted to say. But after the second essay, when my grandmother suggested I needed to think a little further, I realized there are so many things we can do that can't be undone. It has got me thinking a lot."

"I can see that, Amalia. It was not a good thing that you took those DVDs, but I'm glad you have been able to learn so much from this experience."

"So you won't tell my parents?"

"No, I won't tell them. But I think you may want to," and she gave Amalia a thin binder. In it she had placed Amalia's three essays and added a letter she had written explaining what had happened, and how much she felt Amalia had learned from the experience. "I think your parents deserve to know, Amalia, and I also believe you will feel even better after sharing this experience with them. But it will be your decision."

"Thanks, Mrs. Armas. I think I want to do it. It has felt awful keeping a secret from them. But

I will ask my grandmother first. I don't want my parents to be upset with her."

"That's very appropriate, although I can't believe your parents will be upset at all. They will see, I am sure, how much you've grown. But do ask your grandmother. You are very lucky to have such a counselor. She is your true guardian angel."

And Mrs. Armas had been right. Her parents were surprised to hear what had happened. They had never thought their daughter capable of taking something at school without permission. But although they were initially upset, in the end they were pleased to see that Amalia understood she had done wrong, had thought about the consequences of her actions, and had grown from the experience.

The episode did not fade from Amalia's memory. She stopped thinking about it, but once in a while something would bring it back.

At the beginning of last summer, she had gone with her mother to a department store to buy some clothes.

"Do you mind taking a look at things here while I go to try on some shoes? If you see anything you really like, try it on. I probably won't be very long. But if you finish here and I'm not back, you can meet me at the shoe department."

"It's okay, Mom, take your time," Amalia said, anticipating trying on some pants she had been looking at.

Amalia took two pairs of pants and three shirts to the dressing room. One of the pants fit her perfectly and she was very pleased, although the shirts did not look as nice on her as they had looked on the rack. She was about to leave the dressing room when, on removing a skirt that had been left on the bench, she noticed someone's watch under it. It was a very nice watch.

For a moment Amalia thought she could just sneak it into her backpack and nobody would ever know she had found it.

She was about to do it, when she remembered all the thinking she had done while writing those essays. When she came out of the dressing room, she handed the watch to the saleslady.

"I'll call the manager," said the saleslady. "She will take it to the lost and found."

When the manager came, she was very busy speaking on her cell phone. When the saleslady explained that Amalia had found the watch, the manager simply took it and barely nodded before hurrying away.

Amalia felt let down. She had expected to be thanked, maybe even congratulated. But then she realized she had only done what she would have wanted someone to do if the watch had been hers. Nothing special. Nothing requiring thanks or congratulations. Just the right thing to do.

She never told anyone about the little episode, although more than once she thought she would share it with her *abuelita* and they would smile together without the need to say anything. Now that would never be possible.

# 13. Many Voices

The house that had filled with people so quickly now began to empty out. The many neighbors and relatives who had arrived bringing meals had stopped coming after the funeral service, and her aunt and uncles were making definite plans to return to their own lives.

Most of the conversations between Amalia's parents and her aunt and uncles were about planning trips to visit one another, sharing stories about their work, and talking about their children's achievements. No matter how much they talked with one another, there seemed to still be a lot of catching up to do.

Tía Graciela had brought a photo album from Costa Rica, and she kept showing the photos that illustrated all the stories she told of the time when Julián and Lucía were little children.

"If you get me an iPod, Mami, I'll put all your

pictures in it and it will be a lot easier to carry than that big thing," Julián kept reminding her whenever she opened the album.

To Amalia, it seemed they avoided talking about Abuelita, and when they did, it was usually to discuss arrangements or to agree on what to do with her things. It made Amalia very sad to see them disposing of Abuelita's things, but she appreciated it when Tía Amalia brought the lace tablecloth from Abuelita's dining room table and placed it on top of their table. It was the only time she felt some of Abuelita's presence there.

Amalia could see that her relatives were very much enjoying their time together and being a family, but it upset her that they seemed to have forgotten the sad reason why they had gathered.

Antonio, Amalia's father, had not participated much in the exchanges between his wife and her siblings, but one morning at breakfast, he observed, "Do you realize that your mother's last gift to all of you was bringing you all together one more time?"

Realizing the truth of the statement, everyone became silent. A moment later there was much talk among the family about how they were going to keep in touch more frequently now that it was so easy to stay connected with computers.

That evening, during dinner, Tío Patricio and Tía Graciela surprised everyone by announcing they had decided not to return directly to Costa Rica.

"We're taking you up on your invitation, Manuel," said Tío Patricio.

"We'll spend one week at the rancho," added Tía Graciela, who usually completed her husband's remarks. "We've always believed that traveling is the best possible education. The kids will catch up later on the classes they missed."

Tío Patricio then explained, "I think it's a good idea for the kids to get to know the place where we all had such great times when *we* were kids."

"It will give them a true sense of what you have achieved, Manuel," added Tía Graciela.

They were obviously very pleased with the idea of visiting the family rancho, and Julián and Lucía were especially surprised and excited about this unexpected trip.

"We're going to Mexico, to the rancho!" Julián kept repeating. He couldn't contain his enthusiasm. He went on and on, telling his parents how he wanted a pair of boots and a hat like his uncle's.

"You'll let me ride Trueno, Tío Manuel, won't you?" he asked eagerly. Tío Manuel had told them many stories about his two favorite horses, Trueno and Relámpago—that is, Thunder and Lightning. Trueno was a black stallion and Relámpago a golden mare.

"We'll first have to see how good a rider you are," answered Tío Manuel with a smile.

"It's fantastic, isn't it! We get to see the rancho Papá keeps talking about!" Lucía seemed truly excited about the idea.

Her mother had taken her to the mall for the final shopping trip, and she had come home loaded with packages. Lucía had bought presents for some of her friends in Costa Rica and was sure she would be the best-dressed girl in her class.

Tía Amalia was the first to have to return home. She had left Mexico City in the middle of the preparation for a new television series, and she needed to finish her wardrobe designs for the main actors' clothes.

As she explained to Rocío why she could not stay any longer, she insisted that during the summer

Amalia and her mother should visit her in Mexico City.

"We haven't seen each other for so long . . . it's a shame we needed something as sad as this to make us realize we must spend more time together," Tía Amalia said to her sister. And addressing her niece, she added, "It's time you see Mexico City, Amalita. It's an incredible city. There is so much to see. You must come this summer."

Julián added, "Do you realize that there are more than twenty-one million people in the Mexico City metropolitan area? That makes it the largest group of people in this hemisphere. There are more people in the metropolitan area of Mexico City than in those of New York or Los Angeles."

Once he'd found out he was going to the rancho, Julián had been looking up all kinds of information about Mexico on the Internet. "It's the third largest metropolitan area in the world!" he affirmed with great emphasis.

"Numbers are important, of course," Tía Amalia said. "But there is far more than that. In Mexico City, you can see so much of our history. There are the Pyramids of the Sun and the Moon in Tenochtitlan, the capital of the Aztec Empire.

There are magnificent colonial buildings, showing what an important city Mexico was during the colonial times. We will also go to the National Museum of Anthropology, with art from the many cultures that flourished throughout Mexico. And we will see the extraordinary works of the great muralists, especially Diego Rivera, which will help you understand the history of our people. And we will visit the house of Frida Kahlo and the Jardines de Chapultepec. These floating gardens are a reminder that the original city of Tenochtitlan was actually built on a lake."

Julián listened, fascinated. It was clear that he couldn't wait to see such marvels. For Amalia, all of it sounded very distant from her present feelings.

Before leaving, Tía Amalia bought a webcam and installed it on her sister's computer and made everyone promise they would do the same.

She called Amalia's mother the day after she left, and they all talked enthusiastically through the computer.

"You could use this to call Martha sometime," Amalia's mother said to her, after she finished talking to her sister, but Amalia simply shrugged her shoulders. During this awful time Martha's company would have been important to her, but precisely because she would not have had to explain anything. Martha always understood her feelings without her having to elaborate on them. Now, just thinking of having to explain her feelings to Martha was overwhelming. And not something she would like to do over the telephone or the computer.

Amalia continued to feel confused. She could not understand how everyone could feel happy at a time when she felt so miserable and missed her grandmother so badly. The house smelled of food and flowers, and these smells that she normally enjoyed so much now seemed to give her a headache.

She could not stop thinking about that last Friday at her grandmother's. She remembered every moment, every word. And she began to wonder whether her grandmother had been wrong all along, loving everyone so much, when they could just go about their lives so easily now that she was no longer around.

It all seemed very unjust, and it filled her with anger just to think about it.

# 14. Different Experiences

How would you like it if we visited your cousins this summer?" her mother asked the day after everyone had left. It was Saturday and once again, Amalia and her parents were having their slow and lazy breakfast together in the kitchen.

Her father had made a point of gathering branches with bright autumn leaves to place in the center of the table. Amalia appreciated his choice. There had been too many flowers in the house during the last week.

Amalia's mother had prepared an elaborate breakfast with a vegetable omelet, a fruit salad, and Amalia's favorite homemade cinnamon rolls.

"I don't know," responded Amalia, looking at the freshly baked cinnamon rolls, generously drizzled with icing, that she usually liked so much, but that now seemed just plain and boring.

"I know we have been promising to take you

to Puerto Rico to meet your father's family," her mother added. "But your father and I have thought we could go to Puerto Rico during Christmas vacation instead, and let you spend some time with your cousins this summer."

Amalia was silent for a while. It was hard to sort out her feelings. She had wanted to go to Puerto Rico to meet her father's relatives, visit Old San Juan, and above all swim at the beautiful beaches. But it had not occurred to her that her parents would like to travel at Christmas. They had never traveled at that time. That was always a special time with Abuelita. Maybe that was why her parents were proposing it now. Christmas without Abuelita would indeed be very hard. And yet she wasn't sure if what she wanted was more change. As for her cousins, they still puzzled her. She did want to get to know them better, and yet they had seemed so uncaring at a time when she had been so sad.

Finally she said, "I can't believe Julián and Lucía could be so happy . . . you know . . . after what happened." She couldn't find the words to mention her grandmother's death directly, and she realized that she had never said out loud that her grandmother had died.

"After Abuelita died, you mean," suggested her father.

"*Cariño*, your cousins never really had the opportunity to get to know your *abuelita* the way you did, nor share as much with her," her mother added.

Amalia remained silent, watching the butter melt on top of the cinnamon rolls. Somehow, she didn't feel like eating.

Looking at Amalia's plate, her mother got up from the table and said, "I don't feel very much like eating either. Why don't you come with me, Amalita? I have something for you."

Amalia followed her mother silently to the guest bedroom, where she pulled open a dresser drawer and handed Amalia a box.

Amalia recognized it immediately. It was Abuelita's olive-wood box.

"I know how much my mother and you liked to share these cards," her mother said, kissing her forehead.

Amalia nodded and took the box, holding it in both her hands. While Abuelita had shared some of the things in the box with her at different times, she had never seen everything her grandmother kept in it. She could not think of anything she would rather have than this box. Yet somehow she was not sure she should accept it. After all, her mother was Abuelita's daughter. Shouldn't she be the one to keep the box?

"Mami, are you sure you don't want to keep the box yourself? It was so important to Abuelita!"

"*Gracias, amor.* But I have her letters to me and a few other things from her that I treasure. And I suspect she would really like you to have this box. You'll keep it safe, and sometime we can look at it together, maybe at Christmastime." Her eyes swelled at seeing her mother's generosity in Amalia.

"*Gracias, mamá.*" Amalia gave her mother a kiss as she took the box. And when her mother hugged her, a wonderful warmth entered her heart.

She walked slowly to her favorite spot by the window, carrying the olive-wood box very carefully, as if it were a bird fallen from its nest.

# 15. An Unexpected Gift

Amalia looked at the box for a long time without daring to open it.

Having this box meant she would be able to read about some of the things that had been important to Abuelita. One part of the sadness she was experiencing was knowing that she would never hear her grandmother telling her new stories about her life, but now, looking in the box, reading the old cards and letters would be a little like being with Abuelita again.

Finally Amalia opened the box slowly. There, on top of all the cards, was the card that Amalia had drawn for her grandmother last Christmas. It had a bright red Santa surrounded by gifts. She opened it and read the letters covered with silver glitter: *I love you very much*, *Abue*. Her handwriting had certainly improved since last year!

She had not thought about that card all year, but now, looking at it, she remembered how much she had enjoyed creating it. She could almost feel the emotion of when she wrote the card. How wonderful that Abuelita had saved her card!

She wondered what stories Abuelita would have told about her if she had shown the card to Julián and Lucía.

Would she have told them how Amalia had lost her two front teeth on the same day? Or how she had taught Amalia to read using little cards with the names and pictures of her favorite flowers and trees? She knew Abuelita would not have spoken about that difficult time with the DVDs, but would she have shared stories of how much the two of them enjoyed making taffy and licking their fingers afterward?

Amalia smiled for the first time. Just under Amalia's Christmas card was a yellow envelope with her name on it. Amalia's heart lifted as she thought about what could be inside. Slowly she took out the card and saw a forest of trees in the fall with brightly colored leaves.

She opened the card and heard her *abuelita's* voice as she read her handwriting:

*Querida Amalia:*

My heart fills with joy each week when you come to visit.

I thought of you when I saw this card and the way you love sharing family memories with me.

I will always love you and be in your heart. I really love watching you grow up.

*¡Feliz Navidad!*

Abuelita

PS I am enclosing my mother's recipes for pineapple flan and coconut flan. I will enjoy teaching you how to make them just like she taught me, but I wanted you to have these copies of the recipes so that someday you can share them with your grandchildren.

Amalia held a small piece of yellowed paper with elegant handwriting as she brushed off tears with the back of her hand. She placed the card and recipes carefully inside the box again and closed the lid.

She looked at the trees outside the window for a long while, quietly stroking the smooth wooden surface of the box. Although she was crying, this was different. For the first time it felt good to cry.

# 16. A Quiet Sunday Morning

On Sunday morning Amalia was up very early, before her parents. She sat in bed and listened to the silence. After all the visitors during the previous weeks, the house was extremely quiet.

She went downstairs with the olive-wood box held carefully against her chest. She looked at the bare dining room table and laid the box on top of the credenza. She pulled out Abuelita's tablecloth from the drawer where her mother kept the linens. She had seen her *tía* Amalia put it there.

She spread the lace tablecloth over the table and smoothed out all the wrinkles. Then she placed her *abuelita's* box on top of it and went back to her room.

She returned with paper, scissors, colored pencils, and envelopes, and sat down.

All morning she drew and drew.

At some point, her mother placed a plate with a cinnamon roll and a glass of milk next to her and kissed the top of her head without saying anything.

By midday Amalia had completed four cards. One card, in the shape of a snowman with a large mustache, was for Tío Manuel. On the other cards she had drawn two kids on a sleigh for Julián and Lucía, a beautiful wreath covered with ribbons and ornaments for Tía Graciela and Tío Patricio, and a *Nutcracker* ballerina for Tía Amalia.

Her father stopped by for a moment. Noticing how busy she was, he did not stay long but only said, "It seems you'll have some letters to mail. When you're done, let me know. I have to do some errands, and I'll drive you to the post office. We can get stamps from the automatic dispensers."

"*Gracias*, Papi. But I'm not sure if I'll be done today. Maybe we can go another day after school. I haven't written the messages yet."

She could still hear her grandmother say, *I like writing my cards slowly. That way I can really think about what I will write on each one. There are so many things I want to say.*

Amalia remembered that Abuelita always read the cards she had received before writing her own. She opened the box and began looking through every card.

# 17. Colored Leaves

Amalia read and reread cards and letters for the rest of that afternoon. Some were from the previous year, and others from many years ago. She separated out the ones from the relatives who had come to the funeral and a few other people she knew and placed them on top of the table. She left the others inside the box.

Along with good wishes for Christmas or for her birthdays, most every card had words of gratitude. Many of them expressed appreciation for Abuelita's caring and love, and for her concern and advice and the effect that her presence had had in their lives.

After reading the cards, Amalia thought for a while. It seemed that Abuelita treasured knowing that she had made a difference in the lives of others. All of a sudden she could feel in her heart that her *abuelita* was smiling as she taught her another lesson about what is truly important in life.

Amalia continued to look through the box. There was a bundle of letters tied with a bow made of blue ribbon and a simple gold ring tied into the bow. Amalia held the package in her hand but decided to save it for another time.

*Someday I'll ask Mom to explain who some of these people are,* she thought. But now, she wanted to get on with the task she had set out to do.

She went outside. By now, most of the trees were bare. Many of the fallen leaves had been trampled or were broken, but by searching carefully, she was able to find an assortment that were still whole—bright red, golden, maroon, and pale yellow ones.

*I'll send them each a leaf, so they will remember autumns at your house, Abue,* she thought as she went back inside.

# 18. A Mustache Like Zapata's

Sitting at the dining room table, with the bright leaves in front of her, Amalia again read the letters from Tío Manuel. They had been written in Spanish, and when she set out to write, she decided to use Spanish as well.

*Querido Tío:*

Abuelita talked about you all the time. She always said you were a great son.

"Do you know anyone who has returned to do farmwork in Mexico?" she would ask me. "My son did. To take care of our ranch."

She was very proud of you.

I just want you to know she loved you very much. And that she thought you were a great example of honor and loyalty.

The only thing she never told me was that

you had a big mustache like Zapata's. Did you never send her a photo after you let it grow?

I'm sending you a leaf from our backyard, so that you will remember us. And so that you will come back to visit.

*Tu sobrina,*

Amalia

Amalia was happy to see how easy it had been for her to write to her uncle in Spanish and was glad her grandmother had insisted that every time they were together they would read a book in Spanish. *It's not enough to speak a language,* hijita, her grandmother would say. *It's also important to be able to read and write it.*

She stretched her arms and legs. She was tired from sitting down and concentrating so hard.

Just then her mother came into the dining room. Amalia was very glad to hear her say, "You can leave all your things on the table, so you can finish tomorrow. Go, ahead, *hijita*, why don't you change?"

She was even happier when her mother added, "Your dad and I think it would be a good idea to play some miniature golf tonight. You haven't been out of the house for so long."

Amalia rushed upstairs, hardly listening to her mother's last words: "There's a new place where we can play indoors. I'm sure you will like it."

# 19. A Gold Ring

On Monday, when she returned home from school, Amalia went straight to the dining room table. All day she had been thinking about the bundle of letters tied with the blue ribbon and the gold ring.

She pulled on one end of the ribbon and the bow came undone, leaving a heavy worn gold ring in her hand. Amalia saw that the letters were all from Tía Amalia, ordered by date. Tía Amalia had written to her mother right after Amalia's grandfather had died.

She read her aunt's words encouraging Abuelita to follow her own advice, the same advice she had previously given Tía Amalia.

Tía Amalia had been heartbroken after getting a divorce and had given up wanting to do anything. But Abuelita had encouraged her daughter to look ahead, leave her sadness behind, and find new meaning in her life.

Tía Amalia wrote,

> You insisted that I could find a meaning in life. You reminded me how much I had liked to draw clothes, and I came to Mexico and learned to design them . . . and yes, my life is now filled with purpose.
>
> Now it is time for you to do the same. You are so heartbroken because Papá has died, you must find a reason for your life. What about your new grandchild, my namesake? There is so much you will be able to share with her.

Amalia was very surprised. She read the words over and over. They had been written about her. Tía Amalia had been telling Abuelita that she, Amalia, who was a baby then, was a good reason for living.

She rushed to read the following letters. She was mentioned in every one. Tía Amalia would ask about what Abuelita had written. Did Amalita still smile every time Abuelita rocked her in her arms? Her life as a baby unfolded in the comments about how cute she looked with two new front teeth, how excited she had been when she was able to stand up and walk, and how one of her first words had been "Ita"— which, of course, everyone recognized as "Abuelita."

In the last letter of the bundle, Tía Amalia had written, "I'm glad, Mamá, that you have been willing to hear your own words in my voice. And that you have discovered so much meaning in caring for your granddaughter."

Tears filled Amalia's eyes once more, but as her eyes filled, her heart became lighter. She was still so sad that her *abuelita* was no longer there, and she missed her very much, yet it was wonderful to know that she had been so important in her grandmother's life. Thanks to her aunt's letters, she could know for certain how much she had meant to her grandmother at a difficult time. Amalia had been aware of how much she had received from her grandmother. It felt special to know she had also given her something back.

Now, as she looked through the colored leaves on the table, the leaves she had gathered the day before, a very bright red leaf reminded her of the leaf her grandmother had shown her the last afternoon they'd spent together.

Amalia looked at that leaf for a long time. Finally she took another sheet of paper and folded it in two. Outside, she drew a house surrounded by trees, their leaves—golden, yellow, orange, red—shining as bright as the setting sun.

Once she had finished the drawing, she opened the card and wrote in her best handwriting:

> I will always love you very much, very, very much, Abue.
> Thanks for believing that loving me was so important. Your love for me has always been so special, and I am so glad you are still in my heart.
> Amalia

She carefully retied a bow around the letters with the blue ribbon and placed the card for Abuelita on top of all the letters in the box. She slipped the ring onto the necklace she was wearing, closed the box slowly, and went quietly to her room. Her eyes were still moist with tears, but there was a new warm feeling in her heart.

# 20. Soccer Season

During the rest of the week, Amalia spent every afternoon doing homework. After being absent from school for a week, she had a great deal of makeup work to finish. With soccer season starting soon, she needed to be caught up with her homework to have time for practice.

Amalia had thought that without Martha on the team, and without Abuelita and her thermos of hot chocolate to drink after the game, she would not want to play soccer.

"You must not quit. Your *abuelita* would not have wanted to be the reason you quit doing something you love." Her father had been as stern as she had seen him in a long time. "Do you understand?"

"*Sí*, Papi."

Her father hugged Amalia and asked her to go out with him so that they could practice for a while.

"You need exercise, so if you don't play soccer,

you will just have to join another sports team. I promise you that once you are with the team on the soccer field, you will feel like playing. You are really good at it, and you know your *abuelita* loved seeing you happy."

By Friday afternoon Amalia was finally caught up with all the makeup schoolwork. It had been drizzling all day, so she and her father did not practice that afternoon. Instead she put the lace tablecloth on the table and set out to finish the letters to her relatives.

She wrote a few lines on the cards she had drawn for Tío Patricio and Tía Graciela and for Julián and Lucía. She told them how happy she had been to meet them, although she had been so sad about her *abuelita* that it had been hard to show it. She finished by saying that perhaps she would be seeing them in the summer.

Then she started a card for Tía Amalia.

*Querida Tía Amalia:*
    Even though I had not seen you in a long time, you have always been very special to me because I am named after you and because

you are my mother's only sister. She keeps your picture on her dresser and always blows you kisses when she thinks no one sees her.

You are also special because Abuelita spoke so much about you and my mom, when you were little girls.

My father says that Abuelita gave us all one last gift by bringing us together.

Mami gave me Abuelita's olive-wood box, and inside I found some very special gifts. Abuelita had written me a Christmas card for this coming Christmas, and I will cherish that card forever.

Inside the box there was also another gift. This one came from you. I read the letters you sent Abuelita after Abuelito died. It made me feel so good that spending time with me made Abuelita feel better.

*Gracias, Tía Amalia.* You have given me not only my name but also a special understanding of what I meant to Abuelita.

*Te quiero mucho. Tu sobrina, Amalita*

# 21. Still Friends

On Saturday morning, when she got up, Amalia could hear her parents already busy in the kitchen. She dressed quickly, putting on a pair of jeans and her favorite blue shirt. While she was brushing her hair, she looked at the olive-wood box on her dresser. She had cleared everything else from the dresser top so that the box was centered in front of the mirror. She looked at it for a while.

She knew she had been very lucky. That box would remind her every day of a special bond that would never be broken.

And now she had the secret she had learned from Tía Amalia's letter. At a moment of great sadness, she had helped her *abuelita* find a new joy and purpose in life.

She promised herself that she would remember Abuelita's looks, her soft jasmine fragrance, her kind hands . . . and she would carry her words forever.

And then she thought about Abuelita's last words to her: *You will find a way to stay close to Martha.*

During these last weeks, Amalia had not even wanted to think about Martha. The sorrow of losing her grandmother had filled all her thoughts. Slowly she had begun to care about her relatives—those relatives Abuelita had brought to life in her stories were real people who shared more of her history than she ever knew.

Now, remembering Abuelita's words, she thought about Martha. She went to her dresser and pulled open the bottom drawer. There, tucked away under the sweaters, was Martha's envelope. On the top left corner, above her new address, instead of her name Martha had written, *Your best friend.*

Amalia sat down at her desk and put the envelope aside. She would find out what was inside later, but not right now.

Then there would be time to take her parents up on their offer of calling Martha using the computer.

Now she would write one more card. Martha needed to know what had happened to Abuelita before she could talk to her.

She took the golden ink gel pen that had always been Martha's favorite, and she began to write slowly as she thought out her words:

Dearest Martha,

I am very happy we are friends. I remember all the fun we've had and how when I broke my wrist you were my right hand.

Sometimes it's hard to say good-bye, and I am sorry that I was so angry about you leaving that I could not tell you how I felt.

The saddest thing has happened. My *abuelita* is gone forever; she died just a few days after you left. It has been really hard because I never got to say good-bye and tell her how much I loved her.

Everyone says she died very peacefully, just like she had lived. It has been difficult for me to imagine life without her.

Her last words to me were: *You will find a way to stay close to Martha.*

This is why, even though I've been so upset that you left, I'm writing now and have included a very special gold leaf from our yard, since gold is your favorite color.

I miss you a lot at school. It won't be fun to go to soccer practice without you next week. But somehow, even though you are far away, we can find a way to still be best friends.

So I'm going to share a secret with you. The animal shelter where Teresa's mother works is looking for volunteers to foster care for kittens. The volunteers would raise a litter of kittens in their homes, until the kittens are ready to be returned to the agency. Then they put them up for adoption. Teresa brought brochures to school that explain it all.

You know I adore kittens, but I thought it would be crazy to fall in love with a bunch of kittens and then have to give them back. So I just stuffed the flyer in my backpack. I didn't need to lose one more thing I care about.

But now I'm going to ask my parents about giving me a chance. I hope they'll say yes. It's been hard that you moved away, but imagine how sad it would have been to never ever

have had you as a friend. So maybe when you
write back, you can give me a couple of kitten
names you like.

Love,

Amalia

119

# Recipes

You can make the dishes mentioned in
this book by following the recipes below
(with adult supervision, of course!).

## Pineapple-Flavored Flan
### *Flan con sabor de piña*

*Ingredients*

One 14-ounce can sweetened condensed milk

One 12-ounce can evaporated whole milk

2 cups water

One 6-ounce box or two 3-ounce boxes pineapple
 gelatin

1/2 teaspoon salt

*Yields 8 servings*

### Directions

1. Mix the contents of the condensed milk
   and the evaporated milk into a bowl.
   The best way to do this is to first empty
   the entire can of condensed milk into the
   bowl, followed by half of the evaporated

milk. Next, pour the other half of the evaporated milk into the empty condensed milk can and then stir. (This way it will be easier to get all the condensed milk out of the can.) Pour the remaining contents of the condensed milk can into the bowl and stir until the milks are thoroughly combined.

2. Put the two cups of cold water into a pot and bring to a boil. When it is boiling, add the salt.

3. Turn off the heat and then stir in the gelatin until it is completely dissolved.

4. Pour the hot water with the dissolved gelatin very slowly into the bowl of milk, stirring constantly. (It's important to remember to pour the water over the milk if you want a smooth flan. When the milk is poured over the water, it creates lumps.)

5. Continue to stir the mixture till smooth.

6. Cover with plastic wrap and chill in the refrigerator for an hour.

Enjoy!

# Coconut Flan
## *Flan de coco*

### Ingredients

6 whole eggs

6 additional egg yolks

One 14-ounce can sweetened condensed milk

One 12-ounce can evaporated whole milk

One 15-ounce can coconut milk

1 1/2 cups heavy whipping cream

3 teaspoons vanilla extract

2 cups white sugar

1/2 teaspoon salt

1 cup toasted shredded coconut

*Yields 12 servings*

### Directions

1. Preheat oven to 350° F (175° C).
2. Melt one cup sugar in a saucepan over medium heat, stirring with a wooden spoon. When the sugar has melted and is light brown in color, pour into a three-quart glass baking dish. (Make sure to coat the bottom of the pan.)

3. Sprinkle 3/4 cup of the toasted shredded coconut over the warm melted sugar.

4. Make sure the sugar isn't too hot before pressing the coconut firmly into the sugar.

5. In a large bowl, beat the eggs, egg yolks, one cup of sugar, and salt with an electric mixer until smooth.

6. Pour the condensed milk, evaporated milk, coconut milk, whipping cream, and vanilla into the beaten eggs. Mix until well blended, about two minutes.

7. Pour the mixture slowly over the sugar and coconut in the baking dish, then place the dish inside a larger baking dish or pan. Fill the larger pan with about one inch deep of water and set in the preheated oven.

8. Bake for an hour and fifteen minutes in the oven, or until a toothpick inserted in the center comes out clean.

9. Remove the pan of flan from the larger dish. After the flan has cooled, cover the pan with either aluminum foil or plastic wrap, and refrigerate overnight.

10. With a butter knife, loosen edges of flan by running the knife along the sides of the baking dish. Invert the pan onto a serving dish and garnish with the remaining toasted coconut.

# FOR OUR READERS

You can write to Alma Flor Ada
(almaflorada.com)
and/or Gabriel Zubizarreta
(GabrielMZubizarreta.com) to tell them:

1. What do you think was in Martha's package?
2. What do you think Martha's card looked like?
3. What would you put in a package for your best friend if you were moving away?
4. What would be your favorite names for kittens?
5. Have you ever invented a clever guessing game? How do you play it?
6. Do you have a special keepsake? What is it? Who is it from?
7. Has anyone played the role of "guardian angel" in your life? Tell us something about that person.

# A Reading Group Guide
## for
## *Love, Amalia*

**About the Book**

Amalia's best friend, Martha, is moving away, and Amalia is feeling sad and angry. And yet, even when life seems unfair, the loving, wise words of Amalia's *abuelita* have a way of making everything a little bit brighter. Amalia finds great comfort in times shared with her grandmother: cooking, listening to stories and music, learning, and looking through her treasured box of family cards.

But when another loss racks Amalia's life, nothing makes sense anymore. In her sorrow, will Amalia realize just how special she is, even when the ones she loves are no longer near?

From leading voices in Hispanic literature, this thoughtful and touching depiction of one girl's transition through loss and love is available in both English and Spanish.

## Discussion Questions

1. As the novel opens, Amalia's *abuelita* tells her, "You are too quiet, *hijita*. Tell me what's bothering you." Consider her grandmother's ability to detect Amalia's unhappiness: What can be inferred about their relationship through this interaction?

2. Consider Amalia's tradition of going to her grandmother's house each Friday after school. Why does the inclusion of Martha in this ritual make Amalia's grandmother more sensitive to Amalia's sense of loss after Martha's move?

3. Describe Amalia. What makes her a dynamic person?

4. Abuelita tells Amalia, "I know how hard it is when someone you love goes away. One moment you are angry, then you become sad, and then it seems so unbelievable you almost erase it. Then when you realize it is true, the anger and sadness come back all over again, sometimes even more painfully than before." Though she is trying to help Amalia deal with the move of her best friend, in what ways do her grandmother's words foreshadow the profound loss that Amalia will have to experience?

Have you ever had a similar experience where you lost someone with whom you were particularly close? If so, what advice would you give someone dealing with a similar loss?

5. Look at the novel's cover art. In what ways is the image represented symbolic of the events that transpire throughout the course of the book?

6. Why do you think Amalia chooses not to open the package given to her by Martha? Do you agree with her decision? Why or why not?

7. What does Abuelita's focus on saving cards and letters from her family indicate about her character? Do you like to collect similar things from others? If so, what does doing so mean to you?

8. How does Martha's move and Abuelita's death profoundly impact and change Amalia's life?

9. Why does Amalia ultimately choose to tell her grandmother about the theft incident at school before telling her parents? Do you think her grandmother was the best choice? In your opinion, was the principal's punishment fair? What do you think Amalia ultimately learned from the experience?

10. Though grieving the loss of her grandmother is particularly difficult, Amalia realizes she is luckier than her cousins. How is this so? Have you had an opportunity to become close to a grandparent, or another relative outside of your immediate family? If so, what has made that relationship special to you?

11. After the death of her grandmother, how does Amalia uphold the customs and traditions of her *abuelita*? What is it about doing so that makes Amalia feel better? Do you have any traditions or customs that your family follows that are linked to family members who have passed away? What is it about preserving these that is so important?

12. Why does being given Abuelita's olive-wood box serve as a catalyst in changing Amalia's attitude about Martha's move and her grandmother's passing? Do you have a special keepsake that connects you to someone? If so, what is it about that keepsake that makes it so special?

13. Explain the significance of the title, *Love, Amalia*. In your opinion, does it accurately describe the events and relationships portrayed in the book?

14. Using the phrase, "This is a story about . . ." supply five words to describe *Love, Amalia*. Explain your choices.

*Activities and Research*

1. Food plays an important role throughout the novel and in Amalia's relationship with her grandmother. Using the recipes provided at the back of the book, invite a special person in your life to help you prepare one or more of the desserts shared in the book. When finished, take the time to enjoy the company and sweet treats!

2. In our day of e-mails and text messaging, most people no longer write handwritten letters. Consider how Abuelita used her cards to share what others meant to her, and follow her example by creating cards with original art or handwritten letters. Remember, the sentiment (what you are trying to share) is the important part, so be carefree and have fun!

3. In *Love, Amalia*, part of Amalia's story focuses on her connection and relationship with her family and the people that matter the most to her. Think about your own special relationships.

What makes these individuals so important? Compose a personal journal entry where you share your thoughts, and be sure to answer the following questions:

- Who are the individuals who mean the most to you?
- Why are these particular relationships so special?
- What's the greatest sacrifice you've made for the people you love?
- In what ways have the changes you've experienced in your life affected those to whom you are closest?

Share your writing with the group.

4. Consider the variety of settings for *Love, Amalia:* Why is each of these places important to Amalia's development? Using the descriptions provided in the book, illustrate the places you believe to be most important to her story. In addition to the illustrations, include a short explanation of the significance of each, and why you believe it is important.

5. Before Martha leaves, she gives Amalia a thick envelope, likely filled with items to help Amalia remember her by. If you were going

to assemble a similar package for your closest friend, what would the contents be? Create a list of the items you would put inside for her or him and give a reason why each item would be significant to the two of you.

6. Amalia's extended family lives in a variety of interesting places throughout the world. Using the library and the internet, do research to learn more about Mexico City, a typical ranch in Mexico, Costa Rica, and Puerto Rico. If you had your choice, which would you choose to visit and why?

*Guide written by Rose Brock, a teacher, school librarian, and doctoral candidate at Texas Woman's University, specializing in children's and young adult literature.*

*This guide has been provided by Simon & Schuster for classroom, library, and reading group use. It may be reproduced in its entirety or excerpted for these purposes.*

*Even when they don't feel at home, can*
*Margie and Lupe find a way to belong?*
*Turn the page for an excerpt from*
*Alma Flor Ada and Gabriel M. Zubizarreta's*
*moving story of friendship, family,*
*and the classic immigrant experience.*

AVAILABLE NOW FROM
ATHENEUM BOOKS FOR YOUNG READERS

# The Map

Margie felt nervous having to wait outside the principal's office. She kept her eyes fixed on the huge map that covered the entire wall. Mrs. Donaldson seemed to be a pleasant woman, but Margie had never had to address the principal all by herself before.

The map's colors were vivid and bold, showing Canada, the United States, and part of Mexico. Alaska and the rest of the United States were a strong green; Canada was a bright yellow. The remainder of the map, however, showed only a small part of Mexico in a drab sandlike color Margie could not name.

For Margie, maps were an invitation to wonder, a promise that someday she would visit faraway places all over the world.

Looking at this one, Margie could imagine herself admiring the giant glaciers in Alaska, standing in awe in front of the Grand Canyon, gazing at the endless plains of the Midwest, trying to find her way in the midst of bustling New York City, or peering at the rocky coasts of Maine . . . but when her eyes began to wander south of the border, she averted her gaze. *That is not a place I want to visit*, she thought, remembering so many conversations between her parents and their neighbors, tales of families not having enough money to live a decent life, of sick people lacking medical care, and of people losing their land and homes. As she pushed those troubling thoughts aside, Margie's heart once again swelled with pride, knowing she had been born north of that border, in the United States, an American.

Margie looked over at the girl waiting in the other chair outside the principal's office. Her cousin Lupe was not as lucky as Margie, who had been born in the United States. Lupe had just arrived from Mexico and looked completely out of place in that silly frilly dress she had insisted on wearing. "My mother made it especially for me," she had pleaded, and Margie's mother had allowed her to wear it. That dress was much too fancy for school. It was so embarrassing for Margie to be seen with a cousin who was dressed like a doll!

Margie knew her classmates would tease Lupe about her organza dress and her long braids. Would all that teasing spill over to Margie? Were they going to start mocking her, squealing "Maargereeeeeta, Maargereeeeeta" and asking her when had she crossed over from Mexico? She had hated it so much when they used to tease her like that!

It had been such a struggle for Margie to get her classmates to stop thinking of her as Mexican. She was very proud of having been born in Texas. She was as American as anyone else. Now Margie feared that because Lupe was tagging along in that dumb dress, everyone would start back up with the teasing she had hated so much. She could just hear her classmates asking her why she didn't bring burritos for lunch, or looking at her and laughing as they said, "No way, José!"

Margie was still wishing she could have convinced Lupe to dress normally when the principal appeared, walking briskly and motioning for the girls to follow her into her office.

"Good morning, Margarita. What can I do for you?" Mrs. Donaldson's voice was all business. Everything about her seemed to say, *I do not have a minute to spare.*

"Good morning, Mrs. Donaldson. This is my cousin Lupe. She just got here from Mexico. My mother said—"

Mrs. Donaldson, who had begun to shuffle the papers on her desktop, interrupted Margie: "Your mother registered her yesterday, Margarita. Just take her with you to your class."

"To *my* class?" There was surprise and urgency in Margie's voice. "But she just got here. She is from Mexico. She doesn't know how to speak."

Mrs. Donaldson stared at Margie. "You mean she doesn't know how to speak English, right? I imagine she can speak Spanish." Then, turning to Lupe, she slowly said, "*Bien—ve—ni—da* to Fair Oaks, Lupe. *Bonito vestido.*"

Lupe managed a shy smile, but she kept looking down at her feet and answered in the smallest voice, "*Muchas gracias—*"

Margie cut through Lupe's words. "Well, yes, she speaks Spanish. But in my class we only speak English. She is not going to fit in there, Mrs. Donaldson." She was shocked at her audacity in arguing with the principal, but there was no way she was going to show up in class with her Mexican cousin tagging along. Why had Mrs. Donaldson complimented

Lupe's stupid party dress? How could adults be so dishonest? Margie wondered.

Mrs. Donaldson said firmly, "The fifth-grade bilingual class is overbooked. There is no way I can put one more desk in there. Judging by her grades in Mexico, Lupe is a very good student, and since you can help her, both here and at home, we all expect that she will do well in your class." And with a voice that left no room for a reply, she added, "I thought you would be happy about this. She is your cousin, Margarita!"

Mrs. Donaldson looked so stern that Margie decided not to say anything else. She got up and left, signaling Lupe to follow her. But as she was leaving the office, she looked back at the huge map of the United States. This was a great country, and she was very glad that she had been born here and spoke English as well as any of her friends.

Lupe followed Margie down the hall. She had not understood the conversation in the principal's office. It was clear to Lupe that her cousin was upset, but Lupe did not know why. As they made their way to the classroom, everything Lupe saw awakened her curiosity. It was all so different from Mexico! She had never been to a school with so many things hanging on the walls. And she still could not believe that the students didn't wear uniforms. She had been very surprised when her aunt told her. When Lupe arrived in California, Tía Consuelo had bought her some new clothes to wear to school. But for this first day Lupe had wanted to wear the pink organza dress her mother had made. Margie did not seem to like it, but Lupe felt it was important to give a good first impression.

When Margie opened the door, Lupe's surprise grew. They were obviously in a classroom, but instead of the neat rows of desks that she was used to, the students were sitting in small clusters of two or four desks placed around the room. And there were all sorts of different things in the classroom— posters on the walls, mobiles hanging from the ceiling, many different kinds of books on the book- shelves. There was even a fish tank! With binders and backpacks scattered all over, it looked very chaotic, more like a bus station than a classroom.

Stunned, Lupe hesitated in the doorway, afraid to walk in. Glancing at everything from the corners of her eyes, she remembered the neat and orderly classroom of her old school in Mexico. Suddenly she became aware that everyone in the room was looking at her. She dropped her gaze and stared down at the floor in front of her feet.

Meanwhile, Margie went directly to the teacher's desk.

"Miss Jones, this is my cousin Lupe González. Mrs. Donaldson told me to bring her here. But there must be some mistake. She should be in a bilingual class, right?"

The teacher did not answer Margie's question but turned to address Lupe. Margie looked back at Lupe, who had not moved, trying to signal her to come in. Finally, Margie walked back to the door and took hold of her cousin's arm. Lupe jumped a little when Margie grabbed her, and the class was instantly filled with laughter. Lupe raised her eyes and saw that her cousin's face had turned crimson.

Obviously upset, Margie led Lupe over to Miss Jones's desk.

*"Buenos días, Lupe. ¿Cómo estás usted?"* Miss Jones said slowly, pronouncing each syllable of the formal greeting.

Surprised at being addressed so formally, Lupe did not know how to answer the teacher's halting Spanish. But she knew how to show respect, so she looked down. More laughter spread around the room.

"Margie, have your cousin sit next to you, in the back of the class, so that you can translate what I say. That is all the Spanish I know."

"But Miss Jones . . ." The urgency in Margie's voice was greater than ever. "I don't know much Spanish myself. I won't be able to translate everything you say. Besides, I sit up front, next to Liz."

"I have moved you next to the empty seat in the back. That way you can translate while I speak and you won't disturb the rest of the class. Now go sit down, class should have started already. And please tell your cousin that even if she is feeling shy, she needs to look at me when I am talking to her."

Margie sulked toward her new seat, while Lupe continued to stand in front of the teacher's desk. When the laughter started up again, Margie turned and grabbed Lupe, pulling her toward the back of the class. Lupe followed silently. When she dared to look up and smile, the laughter started again, until Miss Jones demanded silence.

While Miss Jones talked on and on about the Pilgrims, Margie searched for the words in Spanish to translate what the teacher was saying. But there was no way she could even begin to convey the half of it, and so she remained silent instead. Lupe looked expectantly at the teacher for a moment, but then she busied herself turning the pages of the history book and looking at the illustrations.

Margie felt deeply hurt. She had always liked sitting up front. And Liz was her best friend. Now she had to sit at the other end of the room, while Betty sat next to Liz. Margie could see them chatting and smiling as if they were already best friends.

Margie had joined in the family excitement when her mother announced that her cousin Lupe was coming to stay with them. Margie had no brothers or sisters, and since none of her school friends lived close by, she thought it might be fun to have someone to hang out with at home. Besides, Lupe could help with the chores—washing and drying dishes and cleaning and straightening the kitchen after dinner would be less boring if the two of them were working together. But above all Margie had hoped that once Lupe was here, it would be easier to convince her mother to let her visit Liz and go out to the mall.

Margie had not thought at all about how having Lupe here might affect her life at school. She had imagined parting ways at the school door, Lupe going to the bilingual classroom and Margie going to her own classroom with her friends.

"Margie! Are you listening to me?" Miss Jones sounded angry. Everyone was staring at Margie, who again felt her face getting warm. "When are you going to start explaining to your cousin what I have been saying?"

"But I told you, Miss Jones. I don't know that much Spanish. I was born in Texas." Margie's voice could hardly be heard, but what could be heard loud and clear was the laughter coming from John and Peter, the two boys sitting on her right.

"Enough!" Miss Jones gave John and Peter one of her silencing looks. "Take out your math workbooks."

Margie felt confused. How could things change so quickly? She had felt so comfortable in this class, and now everything seemed out of control. She looked down at her math workbook, although the numbers looked so blurry that she could hardly read them.